THE WALKING DEAD

SURVIVORS' GUIDE

**TIM DANIEL &
ROBERT KIRKMAN**
story

**CHARLIE ADLARD
& CLIFF RATHBURN**
art

TIM DANIEL
book design

SINA GRACE
edits

THE WALKING DEAD created by ROBERT KIRKMAN

IMAGE COMICS, INC.
Robert Kirkman - chief operating officer
Erik Larsen - chief financial officer
Todd McFarlane - president
Marc Silvestri - chief executive officer
Jim Valentino - vice-president

Eric Stephenson - publisher
Todd Martinez - sales & licensing coordinator
Jennifer de Guzman - pr & marketing director
Branwyn Bigglestone -
Emily Miller - ad
Jamie Parreno -
Sarah deLaine - di
Kevin Yuen - digit
Tyler Shainline -
Drew Gill - art dir
Jonathan Chan -
Monica Garcia -
Vincent Kukua -
Jana Cook - prod
www.imag

SKYBOUND
For SKYBOUND ENTERTAINMENT

THE WALKING DEAD SURVIVORS' GUIDE TP. ISBN: 978-1-60706-181-6. Second Printing. Published by Image Comics, Inc. Office of publication: 2134 Allston Way, 2nd Floor, Berkeley, California 94704. Copyright © 2012 Robert Kirkman LLC. All rights reserved. Originally published in single magazine format as THE WALKING DEAD SURVIVOR'S GUIDE #1-4. THE WALKING DEAD™ (including all prominent characters featured in this issue), its logo and all ss otherwise noted. Image of Image Comics, Inc. All transmitted, in any form thout the express written locales in this publication r dead), events or places, on regarding the CPSIA on 433984

image

AARON

FIRST APPEARANCE: #67
LAST APPEARANCE: NA

STATUS: LIVING
FORMER OCCUPATION: UNKNOWN
CURRENT ROLE: SCOUT, ALEXANDRIA
RELATIONS/ASSOCIATIONS: PARTNER TO ERIC
POINT OF ORIGIN: DISCOVERED RICK & SURVIVORS OUTSIDE OF DC
POINT OF DEPARTURE: UNDETERMINED

LIFE AMONG THEM:

The lead scout of the Alexandria recruitment team. After carefully shadowing and observing Rick's band of survivors with his partner Eric, Aaron declared his presence to the group. He survived both Rick's apprehension and violence and was able to convince the group to follow him back to the colony and find safety behind its walls.

NO WAY OUT:

Once inside the walls, Aaron continued to be a calming influence on Rick, allaying his fears and introducing him to Alexandria's leader Douglas Monroe. Privately, Aaron lobbies Douglas on behalf of the survivors, influencing his leader's decision, allowing them to stay.

ABRAHAM

FIRST APPEARANCE: #53
LAST APPEARANCE: NA

STATUS: LIVIN
FORMER OCCUPATION: SERGEAN
CURRENT ROLE: CONSTRUCTION CREW, ALEXANDRI
RELATIONS/ASSOCIATIONS: PARTNER TO ROSITA, EUGEN
POINT OF ORIGIN: DISCOVERED PRISON SURVIVORS AT GREENE FAMILY FAR
POINT OF DEPARTURE: UNDETERMINE

HERE WE REMAIN:

The former army sergeant was traveling with two companions, Rosita Espinosa and Eugene Porter, when they confronted Rick and his survivors outside the Greene Family Farm following the Woodbury prison slaughter. After a tense standoff, Abraham informed Rick that they were on the road to Washington D.C., to seek answers. With the aid of Eugene's convincing, the two outfits reluctantly merged.

WHAT WE BECOME:

Abraham has proven to be a trustworthy ally, and at times a force of formidible action. On occasion his actions have saved the lives of Rick, Carl and Alexandria resident Holly. In private moments with both Rick and Rosita, Abraham has confessed his regret over his actions, revealing a sensitive nature that belies his outward appearance and often gruff behavior.

ALBERT

FIRST APPEARANCE: #64
LAST APPEARANCE: #66

STATUS: DECEASED
FORMER OCCUPATION: UNKNOWN
CURRENT ROLE: HUNTER, CANNIBAL
RELATIONS/ASSOCIATIONS: CHRIS, DAVID, GREG, THERESA
POINT OF ORIGIN: STALKED RICK'S SURVIVORS OUTSIDE OF GABRIEL'S CHURCH
POINT OF DEPARTURE: KILLED BY ABRAHAM, ANDREA, MICHONNE & RICK

FEAR THE HUNTERS:

One of a small band of cannibals responsible for Dale's abduction and the amputation of his leg.

Dale was taken by two scouts from the hunting party outside Father Gabriel's church where he'd wandered off to die after being bitten by a walker. He did not get far into the surrounding woods when members of Albert's group assaulted him.

Having regained consciousness, Dale revealed to the group that he'd been bitten and was 'tainted meat,' which provoked a strong reaction from Albert, who feared he would 'turn' after consuming a portion of Dale's leg.

The cannibals' bout of stalking the survivors was short-lived, as they were discovered and overwhelmed by Rick, Abraham, Andrea and Michonne. The penalty for their attack upon Dale was severe, as Albert and his band were killed... their remains burned.

ALEXANDER

FIRST APPEARANCE:
LAST APPEARANCE:

STATUS: PRESUMED DECEASED
FORMER OCCUPATION: SECURITY LIAISON, HOUSE OF REPRESENTATIVES
CURRENT ROLE: ALEXANDRIA FOUNDER, ORIGINAL BUILDER OF THE SECURITY WALL
RELATIONS/ASSOCIATIONS: DOUGLAS MONROE
POINT OF ORIGIN: INTRODUCED AS A LEGENDARY FIGURE OF ALEXANDRIA
POINT OF DEPARTURE: PUT OUT OF THE COLONY, HIS ACTUAL STATUS IS UNCERTAIN

LIFE AMONG THEM:

The founder of Alexandria, its original leader and person responsible for the building of the first wall. Alexander Davidson was an enigmatic figure shrouded in mystery by the residents, as even the mention of his name drew a strong reaction. Details of his existence were offered to Rick by new leader Douglas Monroe during a private discussion. According to Douglas, Davidson began to abuse his power as the leader, offering protection to colony women in exchange for sex, or threatening others with expulsion if they did not capitulate to his desires. His rapist tactics led to the suicide of one of his victims, Beth, which clued Douglas into the truth.

TOO FAR GONE:

Douglas also learned that Davidson had intentionally put others in harm's way by taking unnecessary risks or forcing them into risky situations. With little recourse, Douglas burned a walker body, and faked Davidson's death, concealing the truth from the remaining colony members.

Though his headstone occupies the cemetery, Davidson was put out of Alexandria at gunpoint by Douglas and forced never to return.

ALICE

FIRST APPEARANCE: #29
LAST APPEARANCE: #48

STATUS: DECEASED
FORMER OCCUPATION: COLLEGE STUDENT, INTERIOR DESIGN MAJOR
CURRENT ROLE: ASSISTANT TO DOC STEVENS
RELATIONS/ASSOCIATIONS: DOC STEVENS, THE GOVERNOR, RICK
POINT OF ORIGIN: NURSING RICK BACK TO HEALTH
POINT OF DEPARTURE: SHOT IN THE HEAD BY THE GOVERNOR DURING PRISON ASSAULT

THE BEST DEFENSE:

Alice was Doc Stevens' assistant at Woodbury, befriending Rick during his recovery from a severed hand. During his escape, Alice joined Rick and fled to the safety of the prison stronghold.

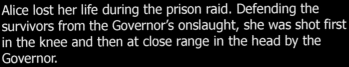

There, Alice sought to study a confined walker for clues to their condition, and to possibly derive a cure. She became an invaluable member of the group when she delivered Lori and Rick's baby, Judith.

Alice lost her life during the prison raid. Defending the survivors from the Governor's onslaught, she was shot first in the knee and then at close range in the head by the Governor.

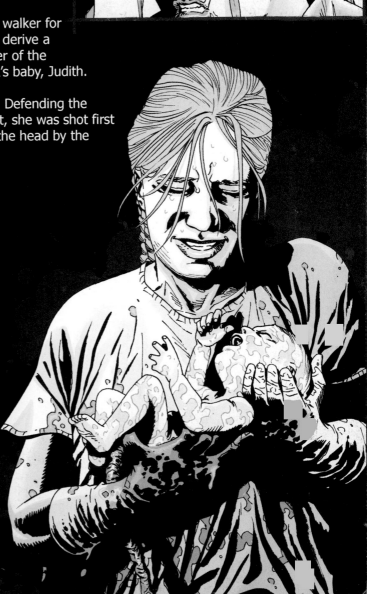

ALLEN

FIRST APPEARANCE: #7
LAST APPEARANCE: #23

STATUS: **DECEASED**
FORMER OCCUPATION: **SHOE SALESMAN**
CURRENT ROLE: **ORIGINAL CAMP MEMBER**
RELATIONS/ASSOCIATIONS: **HUSBAND TO DONNA, FATHER TO BILLY & BEN**
POINT OF ORIGIN: **INTRODUCED AS ORIGINAL CAMP MEMBER**
POINT OF DEPARTURE: **BITTEN BY A ROAMER, DIED DURING FAILED AMPUTATION**

DAYS GONE BYE:

Allen and his family joined up with Dale, Andrea, Amy and Glenn to form the original band of survivors, living in a makeshift camp on the outskirts of Atlanta. Their car broke down on the trip from Gainesville, GA, and they made the remainder of the trip on foot.

Allen always struggled to find his place in the group, never having enjoyed a well defined role, and was often relegated to watching over his twin boys Billy & Ben.

THE HEART'S DESIRE:

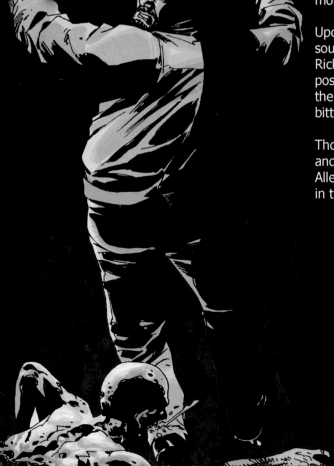

When his wife Donna lost her life during the swarm at Wiltshire Estates, Allen struggled even more as an aggrieved single father.

Upon reaching the confines of the prison, Allen sought to assert himself and volunteered to help Rick and Tyreese clean out Cell Block A of any possible lurking zombies. As the group toured the darkened halls, Allen fell behind and was bitten on the ankle by a lurker.

Though Rick crudely amputated his damaged leg, and Hershel tried to properly dress the wound, Allen succumbed to his injuries, leaving his sons in the care of Andrea and Dale.

AMY

FIRST APPEARANCE:
LAST APPEARANCE:

STATUS: **DECEASED**
FORMER OCCUPATION: **COLLEGE STUDENT, JUNIOR, PHYSICAL EDUCATION MAJOR**
CURRENT ROLE: **ORIGINAL CAMP MEMBER**
RELATIONS/ASSOCIATIONS: **SISTER TO ANDREA, DALE**
POINT OF ORIGIN: **INTRODUCED AS ORIGINAL CAMP MEMBER**
POINT OF DEPARTURE: **BITTEN BY A ROAMER, SHOT BY ANDREA BEFORE SHE COULD TURN**

DAYS GONE BYE:

Amy was returning to college with her sister Andrea when their conditions of living changed dramatically. Broken down and out of gas, the sisters hitched a ride with Dale in his R.V. as he made his journey to the promised safety of Atlanta and his cousins. The trio, along with Glenn, comprised the original camp members.

Upon Rick's arrival at camp, the survivors gathered for an evening meal, all huddled about the campfire, sharing provisions and their personal histories.

During the conversation, Amy excused herself from the group for a bathroom break, and upon exiting the R.V. was overcome by two walkers. She was bitten upon her neck, suffering a lethal wound.

Amy's death, sudden and shocking, meant her sister had to make a gruesome decision. Andrea voluntarily shot Amy in the head before she could turn undead.

ANDREA

FIRST APPEARANCE: #2
LAST APPEARANCE: NA

STATUS: LIVING
FORMER OCCUPATION: UNKNOWN
CURRENT ROLE: SHARP-SHOOTER/SNIPER
RELATIONS/ASSOCIATIONS: SISTER TO AMY, DALE, SURROGATE TO BILLY/BEN, SPENCER
POINT OF ORIGIN: INTRODUCED AS ORIGINAL CAMP MEMBER
POINT OF DEPARTURE: UNDETERMINED

DAYS GONE BYE:

Andrea, a former law clerk, has overcome multiple hardships.
Stranded when returning her sister Amy to college, they
were picked up by Dale and helped form the original survivor
group. Soon thereafter, Andrea would lose Amy to an attack by
a roamer, and make the first hard decision to shoot her sister
before she returned from death.

The ride in the R.V. became so much
more as Andrea first regarded Dale as a
sort of father figure, but found her feelings
had evolved to a romantic level. Comforting,
sound, and rational, Dale was a natural companion
to Andrea's energy and more youthful zeal.

SAFETY BEHIND BARS:

**Andrea began to display a crucial survival skill:
marksmanship.** Acting as the team sentry, her sniper
skills saved the group on several occasions, from various
roamer attacks to human threats. With time available to
the group during their prison stay, Andrea used her shooting
prowess to help teach each of the capable survivors to use
their firearms with good accuracy.

After both Donna and
Allen were lost to attacks
by walkers, Andrea and Dale
assumed responsiblity
for their twin boys,
Ben and Billy, caring
for them with greater
skill and attentiveness
than their own
parents.

THE HEART'S DESIRE:

The prison stay proved physically debilitating to both Andrea and Dale, as each survived serious injury. Andrea successfully fended off a near-lethal encounter with the psychopathic murderer Thomas, a confrontation leaving her scarred from lip to ear. While recovering Andrea nursed Dale back to health after a roamer bite required him to lose his leg below the knee in an emergency amputation.

Sensing a reprisal by the Governor after his first failed attempt to usurp the prison from the survivors, a standoff during which a bullet grazed Andrea's forehead, leaving her unconscious, a recovered Andrea boarded the R.V. along with Dale, Maggie, Glenn, the twins and Sofia, and fled for safety.

Severely undermanned, Rick and the remaining survivors were overwhelmed by the Governor's forces. On the verge of surrender and slaughter, Andrea came crashing into the fray atop the R.V., guns blazing. She managed enough on-target shots against the Governor's army before the R.V. went careening into another vehicle, toppling Andrea from her perch and injuring her.

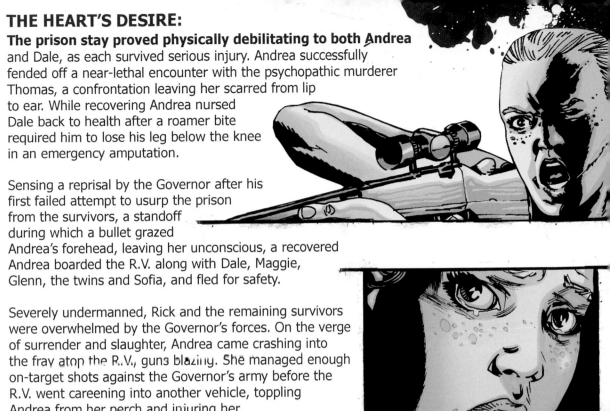

FEAR THE HUNTERS:

Andrea would suffer another loss, when Dale died from a combination of a walker attack and another amputation, this time at the hands of a band of cannibals.

When Dale passed, Andrea was at his bedside and like she had to do with her sister Amy, she pulled the trigger following his death, ensuring that Dale would not return.

NO WAY OUT:

As the lookout for Alexandria, Andrea has been instrumental in fending off one attempted assualt and found brief solace from her mourning of Dale with Spencer Monroe before a falling out.

ANDREW

FIRST APPEARANCE: #13
LAST APPEARANCE: #19

STATUS: DECEASED
FORMER OCCUPATION: DRUG DEALER
CURRENT ROLE: INMATE
RELATIONS/ASSOCIATIONS: PARTNER TO DEXTER, AXEL, THOMAS
POINT OF ORIGIN: DISCOVERED IN PRISON CAFETERIA
POINT OF DEPARTURE: FLED THE JAIL AFTER DEXTER'S FAILED TAKEOVER

SAFETY BEHIND BARS:

Andrew was one of four inmates discovered in the prison during Rick and Tyreese's exploration of the grounds. Andrew and his fellow inmates were dining on meatloaf when Rick and Tyreese burst into the commissary in search of supplies and a safe haven for their fellow survivors.

Convicted for drug possession, selling and theft, Andrew was the cellmate and partner of Dexter, a confessed murderer. When Rachel and Susie Greene were found decapitated, Lori wrongly accused Dexter, confining him to a cell at gunpoint. Andrew later broke into Cell Block A and armed both himself and Dexter with rifles, which they used to make a play to overthrow Rick's authority.

THE HEART'S DESIRE:

Dexter's ploy failed when Rick shot him during a skirmish with several walkers. His partner dead, Andrew surrendered but soon fled the grounds on foot. He is presumed dead.

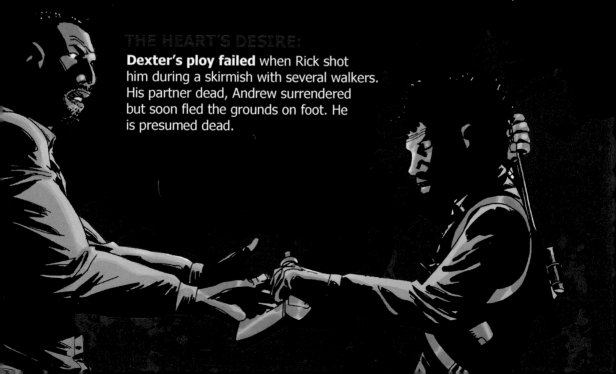

ARNOLD

FIRST APPEARANCE: #10
LAST APPEARANCE: #11

STATUS: DECEASED
FORMER OCCUPATION: FARM HAND
CURRENT ROLE: FARM HAND
RELATIONS/ASSOCIATIONS: SON OF HERSHEL, BROTHER TO LACEY, BILLY MAGGIE, RACHEL, SUSIE
POINT OF ORIGIN: INTRODUCED AT THE GREENE FAMILY FARM
POINT OF DEPARTURE: MAULED BY BITERS HOUSED IN THE BARN

MILES BEHIND US:

The 'one with the chip on his shoulder' as described by his father Hershel, Arnold perished when attacked by his older brother Shawn, who had been turned sometime prior to the survivors' arrival at the farm.

Hershel believed there to be some shred of humanity still remaining in the undead and quite possibly a cure. Instead of killing the walkers he locked those that

wandered onto his property in the barn, including his eldest son. When several broke out and attacked Hershel, Arnold leaped to his father's defense, but was quickly overwhelmed and devoured along with his sister, Lacey.

STATUS: DECEASED
FORMER OCCUPATION: CONVICT, ARMED ROBBERY
CURRENT ROLE: INMATE, LATER MERGED WITH ORIGINAL CAMP MEMBERS
RELATIONS/ASSOCIATIONS: PATRICIA, ANDREW, DEXTER, THOMAS
POINT OF ORIGIN: DISCOVERED IN PRISON CAFETERIA
POINT OF DEPARTURE: SHOT IN THE HEAD DURING GOVERNOR'S PRISON ASSAULT

SAFETY BEHIND BARS:

Axel was one of four inmates discovered in the Woodbury prison commissary as Rick and Tyreese scoured the grounds for supplies and shelter. Affable and at times introspective, Axel overcame any initial skepticism by Rick's group when he attempted to negotiate a truce with his fellow inmate Dexter during a standoff with Rick.

Following Dexter and Thomas's deaths, and Andrew's flight from the prison, Axel became the lone remaining member of the original quartet of convicts. He integrated well into the group through his contributions of labor, wit and courage during a crucial munitions run with several of the survivors.

MADE TO SUFFER:

Axel found fleeting companionship with Patricia, but soon after he was killed when shot in the head during the Governor's final raid upon the prison.

BARBARA

FIRST APPEARANCE: #72
LAST APPEARANCE: NA

STATUS: LIVING
FORMER OCCUPATION: UNKNOWN
CURRENT ROLE: ALEXANDRIA RESIDENT
RELATIONS/ASSOCIATIONS: UNKNOWN
POINT OF ORIGIN: MINGLED WITH MICHONNE AT DINNER PARTY
POINT OF DEPARTURE: UNDETERMINED

LIFE AMONG THEM:

Attempting to ingratiate herself to Michonne at a welcome party for the new members of the community, Barbara offered a bit too much information about the various relationships of her fellow Alexandria residents, even prodding Michonne with suggestions of possible romantic interest.

Her innuendo-laced observations, trivial comments and oblivious concerns quickly frayed Michonne's nerves.

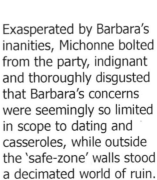

Exasperated by Barbara's inanities, Michonne bolted from the party, indignant and thoroughly disgusted that Barbara's concerns were seemingly so limited in scope to dating and casseroles, while outside the 'safe-zone' walls stood a decimated world of ruin.

BEN

FIRST APPEARANCE:
LAST APPEARANCE:

STATUS: **DECEASED**
FORMER OCCUPATION: **NONE**
CURRENT ROLE: **NONE**
RELATIONS/ASSOCIATIONS: **BROTHER TO BILLY, SON OF ALLEN & DONNA, ANDREA, DALE**
POINT OF ORIGIN: **INTRODUCED AS ORIGINAL CAMP MEMBER**
POINT OF DEPARTURE: **SHOT AND KILLED BY CARL**

MILES BEHIND US:

Ben and his brother Billy endured the deaths of both their parents, Donna and Allen.
Following a roamer attack on their mother at the Wiltshire Estates, Ben and twin brother
Billy were left in the care of their struggling father Allen. Often distracted and forgetful, Allen
neglected his sons. He would suffer a fate similar to his wife and succumb to an emergency
amputation performed by Rick after he was bitten in the prison.

FEAR THE HUNTERS:

Cared for by Andrea and Dale,
the boys seemed to flourish, but
Ben began to show signs of a
disturbed mind, first mutilating a
cat and then later killing his brother
Billy with a knife. His reasoning was
simple - Billy would return to life.
Carl took matters into his own
hands, sneaking into the van where
Ben was confined and shooting him.

BILLY

FIRST APPEARANCE:
LAST APPEARANCE:

STATUS: **DECEASED**
FORMER OCCUPATION: **NONE**
CURRENT ROLE: **NONE**
RELATIONS/ASSOCIATIONS: **BROTHER TO BEN, SON OF ALLEN & DONNA, ANDREA, DALE**
POINT OF ORIGIN: **INTRODUCED AS ORIGINAL CAMP MEMBER**
POINT OF DEPARTURE: **MURDERED AT KNIFEPOINT BY HIS BROTHER BEN**

MILES BEHIND US:

Despite losing both of his parents to roamer attacks,
Billy seemed to enjoy a relatively normal childhood, especially
under the care of Andrea and Dale during their relatively short
tenure at the Greene Family Farm. It was there however,
that Billy discovered Ben had mutilated and killed a barn
cat. His brother threateningly swore Billy to silence.

FEAR THE HUNTERS:

Billy's witness to Ben's cat slaughter was
a sign of his brother's deteriorating mental
state. On the road to Washington, D.C.,
Billy would lose his life in a wooded
roadside area under his brother's knife.
Both his body and a blood-soaked
Ben were found by Andrea.

BILLY

FIRST APPEARANCE: #10
LAST APPEARANCE: #48

STATUS: DECEASED
FORMER OCCUPATION: FARM HAND
CURRENT ROLE: GUNMAN, MERGED WITH ORIGINAL CAMP MEMBERS AT PRISON
RELATIONS/ASSOCIATIONS: SON OF HERSHEL, BROTHER TO LACEY, ARNOLD
MAGGIE, RACHEL, SUSIE
POINT OF ORIGIN: INTRODUCED AT THE GREENE FAMILY FARM
POINT OF DEPARTURE: SHOT IN THE HEAD DURING THE GOVERNOR'S PRISON ASSAULT

MILES BEHIND US:

As Hershel Greene's youngest son, Billy remained
under his father's stern but loving authority until his death
during the prison raid. Billy incurred his father's wrath after
the murder of his sisters, blaming Hershel for joining up
with Rick's group and leaving behind the relative tranquility
of their farm.

Despite their differences, Billy had his father's faith when
he volunteered to fire up the prison generator as Lori
readied for childbirth. With Dale in tow, the two men
rushed to gather more gas for the generator. They were
attacked in the prison parking lot and Billy fled in fear,

abandoning Dale, who had been bitten on
the ankle and knocked unconscious from
the fall. Andrea, returning to the prison,
discovered Billy and assisted Dale to
safety.

MADE TO SUFFER:

Billy never forgave himself. Only a
short time later he was seduced by Carol,
who committed suicide when she allowed
herself to be mauled by a walker.

Caught in a hail of bullets during the Governor's assault, Billy's
hand slipped from his father's grasp as they fled for cover. When
Hershel turned, his youngest son lay dead - shot through the head.

BOB

FIRST APPEARANCE: #29
LAST APPEARANCE: #43

STATUS: PRESUMED LIVING
FORMER OCCUPATION: WAR VETERAN, ARMY MEDIC
CURRENT ROLE: WOODBURY RESIDENT, TOWN DRUNK
RELATIONS/ASSOCIATIONS: THE GOVERNOR
POINT OF ORIGIN: LAYING IN ALLEY INSIDE WOODBURY SECURITY WALL
POINT OF DEPARTURE: UNDETERMINED

THE BEST DEFENSE:

Woodbury resident and one of the few people The Governor showed genuine kindness to, Bob ,a former army medic, suffered from alcoholism. The Governor ensured his care, arranging food and shelter. So familiar were the two, Bob even referred to him as his 'mother hen' when the Governor badgered Bob about is deteriorating appearance, encouraging the town drunk to feed himself.

MADE TO SUFFER:

The Governor's kindness was repaid in full when Bob nursed him back to health following an encounter with a vengeful Michonne. With Doc Stevens dead and Alice having fled, Bob became the last option to save the Governor's life and was forced into doing so by Bruce. Upon his successful recovery, the Governor left Bob to care for his undead daughter as he mounted his final raid upon the prison.

BRUCE

FIRST APPEARANCE: #27
LAST APPEARANCE: #43

STATUS: **DECEASED**
FORMER OCCUPATION: **UNKNOWN**
CURRENT ROLE: **THE GOVERNOR'S MUSCLE**
RELATIONS/ASSOCIATIONS: **THE GOVERNOR, GABE**
POINT OF ORIGIN: **INTRODUCED AT WOODBURY**
POINT OF DEPARTURE: **SHOT IN THE THROAT BY ANDREA IN SUPERSTORE PARKING LOT**

THE BEST DEFENSE:

A key member of the Governor's inner circle, Bruce was the muscle and enforcer. He forcibly pinned Rick's hand to the table as the Governor severed it, then threatened to break Michonne's neck while restraining her as she attacked the Governor and ripped his ear off with her teeth.

Bruce saved the Governor's life when he made a desperate decision and coerced Bob, a former army medic, into treating the Governor's severe wounds following Michonne's violent attack.

MADE TO SUFFER:

Dispatched from Woodbury by a recovered Governor, Bruce intercepted a small group of survivors returning to the prison from a munitions run to the National Guard Depot. He taunted and then shot Glenn but caught a bullet in the neck when Andrea returned fire. There he was left for dead.

The Governor found Bruce clinging to life but past the point of salvation and he expired in the Walmart parking lot but not issuing a warning to his leader. The Governor shot Bruce once in the skull, ensuring that his friend would not return from the dead to walk again.

BRUCE

FIRST APPEARANCE: #69
LAST APPEARANCE: #80

STATUS **DECEASED**
FORMER OCCUPATION **UNKNOWN**
CURRENT ROLE **CONSTRUCTION CREW ALEXANDRIA SECURITY WALL**
RELATIONS/ASSOCIATIONS **ABRAHAM, TOBIN, HOLLY**
POINT OF ORIGIN **INTRODUCED TO ABRAHAM DURING INITIAL CONSTRUCTION SHIFT**
POINT OF DEPARTURE **SWARMED BY WALKERS OUTSIDE THE GATES OF ALEXANDRIA**

LIFE AMONG THEM:

As a member of the Alexandria construction crew, Bruce faced hard labor on the exposed front lines of the 'safe zone'. Abraham was paired with Bruce on his first shift after integrating into the haven and being assigned to construction duty. Alone at the site, Bruce offered some vague bits of history regarding the formation of Alexandria, along with some observations about the nature of their work.

Bruce's harsh words exposed flaws in Douglas Monroe's leadership, his predilection for assigning the hard and dangerous labor to those perceived as the 'most expendable', while other attractive women occupied roles that kept them closest to the colony leader. Abraham's interest was piqued, though he was skeptical and questioned Bruce's opinions.

NO WAY OUT:

On a preemptive clearing sweep of the mass of walkers gathering outside the gates, Bruce was hauled down by several of the undead and bitten severely on the neck and mauled.

Though saved from being completely devoured, he was fatally wounded. With no other recourse to stop Bruce's suffering, Abraham used a a lead pipe to smash his skull before he rose from the dead.

CARL

FIRST APPEARANCE: #2
LAST APPEARANCE: NA

STATUS: LIVING
FORMER OCCUPATION: N/A
CURRENT ROLE: N/A
RELATIONS/ASSOCIATIONS: SON TO RICK & LORI, BROTHER TO JUDITH
POINT OF ORIGIN: INTRODUCED AS ORIGINAL CAMP MEMBER
POINT OF DEPARTURE: UNDETERMINED

DAYS GONE BYE:

Though very young, Carl has grown up very fast. Trained to use a gun for defense, Carl has shown a fierce moral conscience and a deadly proficiency with his firearm. Taken from Cynthiana, KY, to Atlanta by his mother and his father's police officer partner Shane, Carl was an original camp member. Reunited with his father Rick, Carl killed Shane when jealousy drove Shane to the brink of murdering Rick. A secret witness to the confrontation, Carl shot Shane through the neck, saving his father's life. It would not be the last time.

On the move from their camp in search of shelter and supplies, Carl was mistaken for a walker by Otis, a local handyman and resident of Hershel Greene's farm. Carl was taken there and his wound dressed by Hershel. With the remaining Greene family members, Carl and the survivors discovered a prison outside Woodbury. There Carl would see the birth and death of his sister Judith, as well as learn his mother Lori's fate.

MADE TO SUFFER:

As she crossed the prison grounds on foot, cradling her infant daughter, Lori was shot in the torso, a mortal wound killing both her and Judith. Ahead of the fallen mother and daughter, Rick urged Carl on to the safety of the wooded hillside surrounding the prison.

Together, father and son found a suitable abandoned home, and as Rick slowly succumbed to an infection incurred from a gunshot wound to the abdomen, Carl was left to defend the house against a walker invasion. Having experienced so much recent hardship and loss, and fearing his father's seemingly imminent death, Carl's emotions got the best of him.

HERE WE REMAIN:

Carl is resilient and hardened beyond his years. He recovered, as did Rick, and the grief-laden father and son pushed onward but were beset by a horde of walkers that crushed upon their battered El Camino wagon. Michonne reappeared, spearing several of the attackers through the skull and sparing Carl from a deadly mauling.

WHAT WE BECOME:

As the trio traveled on, they were reunited with several members of their group (including Sofia, Billy and Ben), ensconced at Hershel's old farm since the prison fight. A trio of new arrivals led by Abraham would spur the group onward to Washington, D.C., where recent acquaintance Eugene believed salvation awaited.

On the journey, Carl accompanied Rick back to Cynthiana, where he was nearly raped by a trio of marauders. Traumatized by the encounter and his father's intense show of violence in his defense, Carl finally opened up to Rick about his feelings regarding all that he had experienced on the quest for safety.

FEAR THE HUNTERS:

When Ben mutilated his brother with a hunting knife, it was Carl who snuck into the van where he was temporarily confined and shot him in an effort to protect the group against a threat from one of their own.

Shortly thereafter, Rick, Carl and the remaining survivors arrived at Alexandria.

NO WAY OUT:

The walls of Alexandria fell, compromised by the force of thousands of walkers gathered at the enclave's perimeter. With little recourse, Rick fashioned a hasty plan to push his way through the horde beyond the gates. During their plight Douglas fired his gun recklessly into air as he was hauled down and devoured. One of his shots found Carl and his fate now lies in the hands of Doctor Cloyd.

CAROL

FIRST APPEARANCE: #3
LAST APPEARANCE: #42

STATUS: DECEASED
FORMER OCCUPATION: **MOTHER, SOLD TUPPERWARE**
CURRENT ROLE: **ORIGINAL CAMP MEMBER**
RELATIONS/ASSOCIATIONS: **MOTHER OF SOPHIA**
POINT OF ORIGIN: **INTRODUCED AS ORIGINAL CAMP MEMBER**
POINT OF DEPARTURE: **ALLOWED HERSELF TO BE DEVOURED BY A ZOMBIE**

DAYS GONE BYE:

Married to a former salesman, Carol and daughter Sofia journeyed to Atlanta to be with Carol's sister after her husband 'gave up' following his parents' death. They never made it into the city, and joined up with the original camp members.

Shy and guarded, Carol bonded most closely with Lori, playing the role of shoulder-to-lean-on and sounding board. Carol mistook Lori's confidence in her for something greater and propositioned Lori to form a threesome with her and Rick, a notion quickly and strongly rejected by Lori.

THE CALM BEFORE:

Carol enjoyed a short-lived relationship with Tyreese prior to Michonne's arrival, but after she spotted them together, she left Tyreese and propositioned Rick in the same manner she had Lori. The result was the same. Showing signs of mental instability and alienation, Carol seduced Billy Greene. Leaving Billy in his cell, Carol went to the prison yard where Alice kept a biter tied to a post for the purpose of study, and allowed herself to be devoured.

Carol's daughter Sofia was left in the care of Maggie and Glenn.

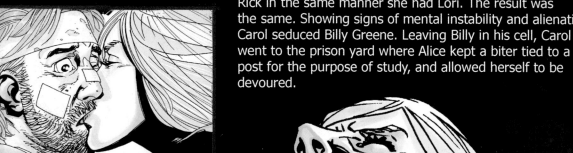

CHRIS

FIRST APPEARANCE: #7
LAST APPEARANCE: #15

STATUS: DECEASED
FORMER OCCUPATION: UNKNOWN
CURRENT ROLE: MERGED WITH ORIGINAL CAMP MEMBERS DURING PRISON STAY
RELATIONS/ASSOCIATIONS: BOYFRIEND TO JULIE, TYREESE
POINT OF ORIGIN: INTRODUCED AS MEMBER OF TYREESE'S SURVIVOR HERD
POINT OF DEPARTURE: STRANGLED TO DEATH BY TYREESE

MILES BEHIND US:

Traveling at night on foot, Chris was part of a trio of survivors led by Tyreese that emerged from the darkness and startled Rick while he, Glenn and Allen struggled to clear the roadway of an abandoned vehicle.

Introduced by Tyreese as his daughter's boyfriend, Chris had been staying with Tyreese and Julie at the outset of the crisis due to a troubled situation at his own home.

Starving, freezing and without shelter or transportation, Rick allowed the trio to join the group. After the discovery of the Greene Family Farm and a subsequent attack by walkers sequestered in the barn left several Greene family members dead, the group began training with firearms to better ensure their own protection.

Tyreese allowed Chris and Julie to remain in possession of their guns following the training - a decision that enabled the young couple to further their plans to carry out a secret pact.

SAFETY BEHIND BARS:

Inside the prison walls, Chris and Julie were relegated to supervising the children as Rick and Tyreese secured the grounds. Frustrated with this duty, Chris began to display an erratic temper.

Later, after lovemaking, Chris and Julie sat cross-legged and naked, guns drawn. They intended to carry out a double suicide, but Chris shot first, mortally wounding Julie. The shot brought Tyreese scrambling to his now dead daughter's aid. Chris looked on with growing horror as Julie turned undead. Struggling to fend off his emotions and his ravenous daughter, Tyreese flew into a rage when Chris' second shot once again terminated Julie's life.

Tyreese strangled Chris to death only to allow him to turn so Tyreese could kill him again, this time more slowly. As he promised Rick, Tyreese burned Chris and Julie's bodies in the prison yard the following morning.

CHRIS

FIRST APPEARANCE: #63
LAST APPEARANCE: #66

STATUS: **DECEASED**
FORMER OCCUPATION: **UNKNOWN**
CURRENT ROLE: **LEADER OF THE HUNTER/CANNIBALS**
RELATIONS/ASSOCIATIONS: **ALBERT, DAVID, GREG, THERESA**
POINT OF ORIGIN: **INTRODUCED AFTER DALE'S CAPTURE**
POINT OF DEPARTURE: **KILLED BY ABRAHAM, ANDREA, MICHONNE & RICK**

FEAR THE HUNTERS:

With supplies running out and wild game hard to track, Chris made a decision; locating and killing humans as a food source was a more efficient method of self-preservation. First, however, there was the issue of the surviving children...so Chris confessed upon being confronted by Rick.

Before long, human flesh became a standard means of sustenance: select a solitary traveler or small group, engender their trust, murder and eat them. If not track the unsuspecting victim like a wild animal and take them through an ambush. Recently, however targets of this variety had become scarce and infrequent. When Rick's sizable group of survivors move through the area, settling at Father Gabriel's church, Chris dispatched two scouts to ascertain their number and select a potential victim.

Weakened by a walker's bite and fearing he might turn at any time, Dale abandoned the group, decidi it best to disappear into the surrounding woods. He did not get far before Chris's scouts greeted him with the butt of a rifle. When he awoke, Dale's lower left leg had been removed and the hunters were feasting around an open fire, a hunk of Dale's flesh roasting on the spit. Dale had the last gh, revealing his walker bite to the group and warning them all they were consuming 'tainted meat' as Chris and his fellow hunters dined upon what was once Dale's lower leg.

The revolting truth inspired the hunters to dump Dale back at the church. To unnerve the survivors, they fired a shot into Glenn's leg. Abraham correctly figured the purpose of the shot was to spook them. Dale provided some vague clues as to where he had been kept during his abduction.

Rick, Michonne, Andrea, Abraham and Father Gabriel located Chris's shelter and confronted the cannibals. The two leaders engaged in a tense standoff. Rick had positioned Andrea out of the lin of sight. She deftly winged Greg, the muscle of the group, then removed Chris's finger with her second shot. Abraham confiscated the weapons, while Chris, on his knees beaten and bloodied, pleaded mercy, only moments before he had threatened Rick with an 'eat or be eaten' bravado.

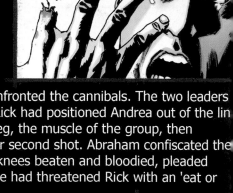

Rick gave no quarter, and with the help of his fellow survivors, Chris and each member of his hunting party were executed, their remains burned...

DALE

FIRST APPEARANCE:
LAST APPEARANCE:

STATUS: DECEASED
FORMER OCCUPATION: SALESMAN
CURRENT ROLE: ELDER STATESMAN, LOOK OUT, SURROGATE FATHER
RELATIONS/ASSOCIATIONS: PARTNER TO ANDREA, SURROGATE FATHER FOR BEN & BILLY, AMY, RICK, CHRIS
POINT OF ORIGIN: ORIGINAL CAMP SURVIVOR
POINT OF DEPARTURE: DIED FROM WALKER BITE & CANNIBAL ATTACK

DAYS GONE BYE:

Using his R.V. camper as shelter and having the calm wisdom of an elder statesman, Dale was one of the original camp survivors. Prior to the outbreak he was a salesman. Having spent forty years as a desk jockey working the phones, Dale and his wife purchased the camper upon his retirement and set out to see America. En route from Florida to Atlanta to visit his cousins, the undead claimed his wife's life. On the road, Dale discovered sisters Amy and Andrea. They were joined by Glenn, Jim, Allen, Donna and their twin boys. Soon thereafter, Shane, Lori and Carl arrived and following Rick's miraculous appearance, what was the original group was formed. Being in a rural area on the outskirts of Atlanta meant guarding against the constant threat of attack, which eventually occurred when Dale saved Donna's life by beheading a walker with an axe. This initial skirmish was a prelude to a subsequent attack that claimed Amy's life and soon thereafter, Jim's as well.

MILES BEHIND US:

Dale and Rick forged a father and son-like bond; often respectful, sometimes tense. This was first evident when Dale attempted to discuss Shane and Lori's relationship with Rick. Rick flashed his temper, cutting Dale off, while Dale embraced Rick with an apologetic and reassuring hug. Now threatened by their surroundings, the group piled into Dale's R.V. He helmed the wheel, steering them to Wiltshire Estates. Exploring the grounds, Dale stumbled upon a semi-frozen walker, scaring the group and, most of all, Andrea. Her reaction to the incident proved a tip-off to their blossoming romance, when later that evening Donna discovered them making love. At Hershel's Farm, Dale confirmed his love to Andrea, reassuring her that although he still grieved for his recently deceased wife, he genuinely cared for her.

SAFETY BEHIND BARS:

The relocation to a prison outside Woodbury proved particularly costly to both Dale and Andrea. She was attacked and nearly killed by a psychopathic inmate and he had the difficult task of talking some reason into Rick, who was suffering with the pressures of leadership.

THE HEART'S DESIRE:

Feeling the duress of their stay, Andrea privately raised the idea to Dale that maybe the greatest threat was not from the undead but other humans seeking to take their prison sanctuary by force...

THE CALM BEFORE:

With Lori on the verge of childbirth and the prison's generator sputtering, Billy recruited Dale to help him siphon gas from the cars in the staff lot in order to keep the power running. Out in the darkness, Dale was caught off guard by a biter, having concealed itself under one of the vehicles. Andrea and Axel, returning from a munitions run, discovered that Dale had been gouged on the right ankle and he was rushed to the infirmary. Alice could not bring herself to amputate Dale's leg. Hershel and Rick were forced to perform the emergency removal of Dale's lower right leg with a bone saw and no anesthesia.

MADE TO SUFFER:

Andrea's suspicion that the prison would make them a target was realized in the person of the Governor. After the survivors repelled his first assault, Dale and Andrea (now caring for Ben and Billy), fled the prison in the R.V., taking Glenn and Maggie with them to safety. At the height of the second battle with all hope seemingly lost, Dale crashed the R.V. into the melee with Andrea on the roof, rifle in hand. She quickly turned the tide with several well placed shots. The Governor's forces rammed the R.V. with a truck and Andrea was injured, but not before they had helped save several of their fellow survivors.

WHAT WE BECOME:

The remaining survivors eventually gathered at Hershel's Farm. Dale attempted to convince Andrea to make a life there, but she continued to question the wisdom of making a stationary camp and prevailed upon Dale to go on the road once more. Without the R.V., the group traveled in a large open-bed munitions truck obtained from the National Guard Depot.

FEAR THE HUNTERS:

The road was cruel to Dale. The journey's first horrific turn came when Ben murdered his brother Billy. Immediately on the heels of this, Carl shot and killed Ben. Only Morgan bore witness to the act; Dale never learned the truth. When their temporary home was overrun by several roamers, Dale was cut off from the group and bitten severely on the shoulder. He lied to the group about the bite, claiming that the walker only startled him and tore his shirt. But under the cover of darkness, he snuck off into the woods, knowing he'd soon show the telltale signs of the undead. Only a few steps from camp, Dale was struck by the butt of a rifle and hauled off by two strangers. When Dale regained consciousness he learned that his abductors were cannibals. They had severed his left lower leg and were roasting it over an open fire. Dale offered them a surprise of his own, revealing his bite wound. His cries of 'tainted meat' spooked the cannibals and they returned him to his fellow survivors. There in Father Gabriel's church, Dale succumbed to his wounds and died, comforted by Andrea who dutifully shot him before he turned undead.

DAVID

FIRST APPEARANCE: #64
LAST APPEARANCE: #66

STATUS: **DECEASED**
FORMER OCCUPATION: **UNKNOWN**
CURRENT ROLE: **HUNTER, CANNIBAL**
RELATIONS/ASSOCIATIONS: **ALBERT, CHRIS, GREG, THERESA**
POINT OF ORIGIN: **INTRODUCED FOLLOWING DALE'S CAPTURE**
POINT OF DEPARTURE: **KILLED BY ABRAHAM, ANDREA, MICHONNE & RICK**

FEAR THE HUNTERS:

A member of the cannibalistic hunting party that preyed upon humans passing through the region.

David and his five fellow hunters carefully stalked Rick's group as they took refuge close by in Father Gabriel's church. Recognizing that they were outnumbered by Rick's party, the hunters awaited the opportunity to isolate a victim. The cannibals observed their habits, stalking the perimeter of the churchyard, remaining in the shadows of the nearby woods.

The hunters struck when, following a bite by a roamer, Dale abandoned Father Gabriel's church. Knowing he would soon turn, Dale sought to die alone in the woods. He was struck by the butt of a rifle and was carried off by two scouts.

Dale's lower leg was amputated and roasted over an open fire. When he later regained consciousness Dale revealed that he'd been bitten and was 'tainted meat.' In their revulsion, the cannibals panicked. David proved the voice of reason, suggesting they all remain calm and rationally note that the meat had been fully cooked. There was little or no indication that Dale's condition would have any effect upon them. Nevertheless, Dale was returned, dropped unconscious in the churchyard.

Using some clues from Dale, Rick and several of his fellow survivors tracked the hunters back to their shelter. When confronted by Rick, Chris recounted their tale and the conditions that ultimately led them to cannibalism.

He then foolishly threatened Rick and all of the survivors with the same fate as Dale.

Rick was prepared, having placed Andrea out of the line of sight as an insurance against an attack.

In retaliation, Rick signaled to Andrea to open fire. Two precise shots ended the confrontation. After their firearms where taken by Abraham, David and the other hunters were executed and their remains burned.

DENISE

FIRST APPEARANCE: #71
LAST APPEARANCE: NA

STATUS: LIVING
FORMER OCCUPATION: GENERAL PRACTICIONER
CURRENT ROLE: GENERAL PRACTICIONER-SURGEON, ALEXANDRIA
RELATIONS/ASSOCIATIONS: HEATH, SCOTT, DOUGLAS
POINT OF ORIGIN: INTRODUCED AS A DOCTOR WHEN TREATING SCOTT'S SHATTERED LEG
POINT OF DEPARTURE: UNDETERMINED

LIFE AMONG THEM:

An invaluable member of Alexandria, Doctor Denise Cloyd provided a general practitioner care to the community. Her rare skill was seemingly always in high demand as is evident when she was introduced to Rick and his survivors upon their arrival at Alexandria. Denise was pressed into work, attempting to salvage Scott's severely damaged leg, an injury he sustained during a fall on a scouting mission.

As she nursed his injury, Denise befriended Scott's scouting partner, Heath, and the doctor and scout become intimate as Heath kept a steady vigil at his fallen partner's bedside. Heath took comfort from Denise as Scott's health declined due to complications from the injury. Denise was once more pressed into service after Rick confronted Pete, their fight leading to injuries to both parties.

NO WAY OUT:

She could barely catch a breath after Scott's passing when Aaron arrived on horseback from a scouting run with a wounded Eric. Denise successfully treated a stab wound Eric received in a confrontation with an unknown woman lurking outside the Alexandria walls.

Her respite was short lived as the walls of Alexandria fell and walkers poured through the streets. She first dressed Morgan's amputated arm, but during a botched escape attempt, Carl is shot through the eye - the stray bullet from Douglas's gun taking a good portion of the right-side of his skull. In a frantic attempt to save his live, Rick left a dying Carl in her capable hands, forcing Denise to attempt her most challenging procedure yet.

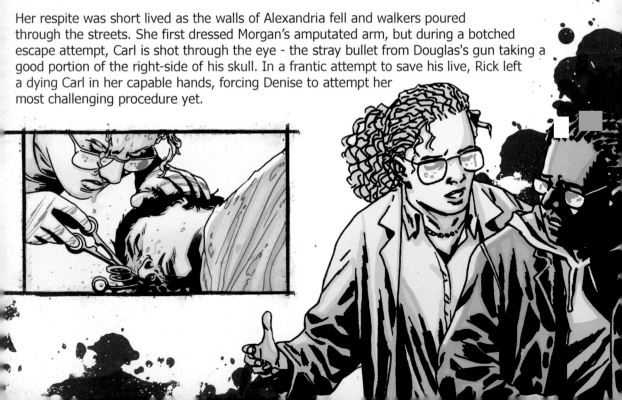

DEREK

FIRST APPEARANCE: ##73
LAST APPEARANCE: ##78

STATUS: DECEASED
FORMER OCCUPATION: UNKNOWN
CURRENT ROLE: LEADER OF A BAND OF SCAVENGERS SEARCHING FOR ALEXANDRIA
RELATIONS/ASSOCIATIONS: RICK
POINT OF ORIGIN: SPOTTED BY HEATH & GLENN IN WASHINGTON D.C.
POINT OF DEPARTURE: SHOT IN THE HEAD OUTSIDE THE GATES BY ANDREA

TOO FAR GONE:

The leader of a band of scavengers trapped inside of a building in Washington, D.C. for more than a week. Derek and his small band were spotted by Heath and Glenn, who were camped out on a nearby rooftop, a temporary rest-stop during a medical supply run. There, they witnessed Derek lead a charge through the streets by feeding one of his group members to the hordes of undead gathered outside the building. Derek traced the sound of Heath and Glenn's motorcycles as they bolted the city and fought through the mobbed streets of D.C. in hopes of locating the much-rumored safe-zone. Derek's quest was furthered when the report of Rick's shooting of Pete echoed beyond Alexandria's walls. Locating the general direction of the gunshot, Derek steered the group to the locked gates of the sanctuary and there demanded entrance.

Yet he was stonewalled by a very leery Rick. Having lived through the Governor's prison massacre, Rick was in no way eager to allow Derek to strong-arm his way into their newfound home. Derek countered Rick's refusal with a series of threats. In response, Rick signaled to Andrea, who was secretly positioned high above them in a clock tower. A highly skilled sniper, Andrea shot Derek through the head, killing him. With their leader dead on the ground before them, the group retaliated in full force. Their assault was short-lived, countered by several additional Alexandria residents, allowing Rick to successfully defend the community by swiftly eliminating the threat.

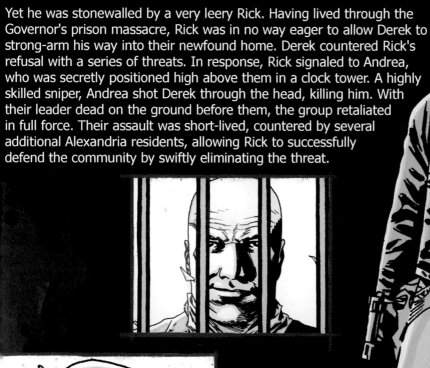

DEXTER

FIRST APPEARANCE: #13
LAST APPEARANCE: #18

STATUS: **DECEASED**
FORMER OCCUPATION: **MURDERER**
CURRENT ROLE: **INMATE**
RELATIONS/ASSOCIATIONS: **PARTNER TO ANDREW, AXEL, THOMAS**
POINT OF ORIGIN: **DISCOVERED LOCKED IN THE PRISON CAFETERIA**
POINT OF DEPARTURE: **SHOT IN THE HEAD BY RICK**

SAFETY BEHIND BARS:

One of four convicts discovered by Rick and Tyreese during their exploration of the prison grounds. Found quietly dining on meatloaf in the cafeteria, Dexter confessed that he was convicted prior to outbreak for the murder of his wife and her lover, though he swears that their deaths were the last by his hand.

During the intervening days it became apparent that Dexter and Andrew - another fellow convict and former cell mate - had formed a relationship of sexual convenience and a close bond of trust. Dexter was by far the most physically imposing of the foursome, though his demeanor was pleasant and openly friendly. He professed his trust of Rick and the survivors and agreed to share the prison with them.

His acceptance abruptly ended when Hershel's twin girls were found beheaded. Panicked, Lori wrongly accused Dexter of their murder, and forced him at gunpoint, with Dale's aid, into a locked cell. As the group soon learned, Thomas was responsible for the deaths of Hershel's girls. Despite the truth, Dexter received no apology from the survivors and they only appeared even more suspicious of the innocent man. Seething with rage, Dexter mounted a plot for revenge, dispatching Andrew to the armory to retrieve guns. His partner returned with the firearms and set Dexter free.

THE HEART'S DESIRE:

Together they made a play to oust Rick and his people from the prison. The ploy was interrupted when the fences failed and the grounds were overrun with the undead.

During the height of the skirmish, Rick used the cover of the gunfire to shoot Dexter in the head, killing him. Outmanned and outgunned, Andrew surrendered his rifle to Tyreese.

"DOC" STEVENS

FIRST APPEARANCE:
LAST APPEARANCE:

STATUS: **DECEASED**
FORMER OCCUPATION: **SURGEON**
CURRENT ROLE: **GENERAL PRACTICIONER-SURGEON, WOODBURY**
RELATIONS/ASSOCIATIONS: **THE GOVERNOR, ALICE, BRUCE, GABE, RICK**
POINT OF ORIGIN: **INTRODUCED AS SURGEON AFTER THE GOVERNOR SEVERED RICK'S HAND**
POINT OF DEPARTURE: **BITTEN BY A ZOMBIE WHILE ESCAPING WOODBURY**

THE BEST DEFENSE:

Summoned from his sleep late one evening,
"Doc" Stevens arrived at the Woodbury infirmary in the middle of a crisis. The Governor's ear was badly mangled, and a stranger dressed in riot gear who was missing his right hand was dying on a gurney beside him. The Governor ordered Stevens to stop the man's bleeding, insisting that he be saved, because as the Governor explained, the stranger had something of value. Stevens sarcastically challenged the Governor's authority, but fulfilled his order. With the assistance of Alice, a young woman who Stevens had been training in the medical practice, Stevens saved Rick's life. When Rick regained consciousness, he attacked Doctor Stevens, and was quickly sedated. When Rick awoke once again - this time in a calmer state - Stevens took the opportunity to explain to Rick that the Governor was once a good man, a man willing to do anything to protect the survivors in the Woodbury community, but that it soon became apparent that the Governor was simply a malicious leader, capable of unspeakable atrocities. The citizenry of Woodbury - including Doc Stevens - were terrified of the Governor's leadership, but never opposed his authority for fear of retribution.

THIS SORROWFUL LIFE:

Healed enough to travel, Rick joined Michonne and a Woodbury defector named Martinez. On their way out of the safe-zone, they recruited the kindly Doctor and his assistant. Together, they fled over the wall, but just outside of Woodbury, Doc Stevens was hauled down by a walker and bitten. Before Alice could shoot him, Stevens pleaded for her to view his transition to becoming undead as merely a form of evolution. Drawing his last breath, Stevens encouraged Alice to take his medical bag and use the knowledge he had given her over the last several months to care for the survivors.

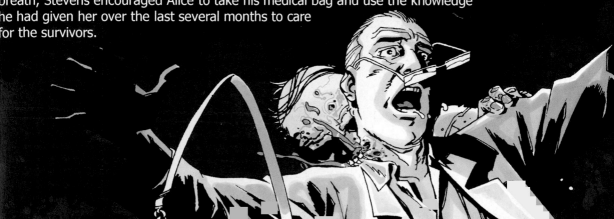

DONNA

FIRST APPEARANCE: #3
LAST APPEARANCE: #9

STATUS: **DECEASED**
FORMER OCCUPATION: **HOUSEWIFE**
CURRENT ROLE: **MOTHER & WIFE**
RELATIONS/ASSOCIATIONS: **WIFE TO ALLEN, MOTHER TO BILLY & BEN**
POINT OF ORIGIN: **INTRODUCED AS ORIGINAL CAMP MEMBER**
POINT OF DEPARTURE: **DEVOURED BY ROAMERS AT WILTSHIRE ESTATES**

DAYS GONE BY:

A housewife, mother and Tupperware representative, Donna and her husband Allen struggled with bills and the responsibilities of raising a family as his shoe store business teetered on the verge of bankruptcy.

Donna, Allen and their twin boys Ben and Billy joined up with Dale, Andrea, Amy and Glenn to form the original band of survivors living in a makeshift camp on the outskirts of Atlanta. On the trip from Gainesville, GA, their car broke down, forcing Donna and her family to make the remainder of the trip on foot.

As an elder member of the survivors, several years her husband's senior, Donna was quick to offer her often strong opinions. She balanced her outspoken nature with performing routine domestic tasks stereotypically associated with women, a role she did not always agree with, and an outmoded notion of femininity she expressed disdain towards.

MILES BEHIND US:

The survivors broke camp after an attack by several walkers devastated their ranks, claiming the lives of Amy and later Jim. Donna, Allen and the twins piled into Dale's R.V. once more, as the entire group headed out on the open road in search of reliable shelter. The onset of winter brought the first snow, and on a frigid morning the group pulled up to the promising gates of Wiltshire Estates. The private community of spacious homes protected from the world by high concrete walls.

After a cursory sweep through a couple of dwellings, Rick and Tyreese cleaned out what appeared to be no more than a few straggling roamers. The survivors bedded down in their new homes.

A brilliant sunrise greeted the survivors the followir morning. Rising temperatures quickly melted snow that had accumulated in the days prior. As they ros from their beds, finding their footing with unfamilia morning routines, an unseen warning appeared on the walls of the community, 'All Dead, Do Not Enter

Wiltshire Estates was overrun, the undead pouring forth from the surrounding neighborhood as they detected the sounds and smells of the living. The survivors where swarmed and as they made a run for the R.V., the horde devoured Donna.

DOUGLAS

FIRST APPEARANCE:
LAST APPEARANCE:

STATUS: DECEASED
FORMER OCCUPATION: CONGRESSMAN
CURRENT ROLE: LEADER OF ALEXANDRIA
RELATIONS/ASSOCIATIONS: HUSBAND TO REGINA, FATHER TO SPENCER, TOBIN
POINT OF ORIGIN: INTRODUCED BY AARON AS LEADER THE ALEXANDRIA
POINT OF DEPARTURE: SWARMED AND DEVOURED BY WALKERS

LIFE AMONG THEM:

A former congressmen, and Democratic representative from the second District of Ohio, Douglas Monroe lived in the open for three months before arriving at Alexandria. The community founder, Alexander Davidson, was a respectable man whose motives as a leader pushed Douglas to call him into question. After learning that Davidson raped a young woman who then committed suicide, Douglas forced him from the community at gunpoint, and assumed the leadership role. The toll of leadership soon began to tell upon Douglas. His own methods of duty assignment - surrounding himself with the attractive young female members of the community - showed that he shared more in common with Davidson than he may have suspected of himself. Despite all of this, Douglas welcomed Rick's survivors into the community, providing them with housing, food and roles that fit their talents. He did not hesitate to speak his mind, sometimes often forcibly to Rick as well as other more familiar Alexandria residents. He upbraided Heath and Father Gabriel for speaking out against Rick, but took Aaron's counsel about the new survivor's character. Although he was married to Regina, and a father to their adult son Spencer, that did not seem to stop Douglas from secretly propositioning Andrea.

TOO FAR GONE:

Perhaps Douglas' motive for standing by Rick was evident in the aftermath of several deaths, concluding with the loss of his wife Regina. In a private discussion, Douglas abdicated his authority to Rick, claiming that he was no longer fit to lead, and that Rick was able to foresee traits in people and organize their defense against threats Douglas was no longer capable of handling.

NO WAY OUT:

Grieving the loss of his wife, Douglas shuttered himself inside his home. The security wall collapsed under the weight of numerous undead that gathered against the barrier. Douglas watched in horror from the confines of his home as the walkers streamed through the streets and devoured several members of Rick's party who were attempting to escape. Wading into the chaos, gun drawn, Douglas began firing wildly. He was grounded and devoured before Rick could save him. One of his misfires hit Carl in the eye, severely wounding him.

DUANE

FIRST APPEARANCE: #1
LAST APPEARANCE: #58

STATUS: DECEASED
FORMER OCCUPATION: N/A
CURRENT ROLE: N/A
RELATIONS/ASSOCIATIONS: SON OF MORGAN
POINT OF ORIGIN: ASSAULTED RICK WITH A SHOVEL, MISTAKING HIM FOR A ROAMER
POINT OF DEPARTURE: DUANE WAS SWARMED, BITTEN, AND TURNED UNDEAD

DAYS GONE BY:

A well placed shovel strike to back of his head served as Rick Grimes' first human contact since awakening from his coma. Duane Jones and his father Morgan had appropriated Rick's former neighbor's home and Duane, mistaking Rick for a roamer, attacked him with a shovel, knocking Rick unconscious.

THIS SORROWFUL LIFE:

Unsure of the calendar, Duane enjoyed a surprise from his father when Morgan staged an impromptu Christmas. Having exhausted his comics and growing bored, Duane was overjoyed to receive a working Gameboy, plus games and fully-juiced batteries. The sight of Duane preoccupied with his new toy brought Morgan to tears of joy as he lamented their solitude.

WHAT WE BECOME:

When Rick revisited his old neighborhood, he was greeted once again by a shovel to the head, this time from an emaciated Morgan. Rick learned that some three months prior, Duane had been attacked, bitten and turned undead. Unable to cope with the loss of his son, Morgan had been killing strangers and dogs, feeding them to Duane, hoping against hope to see some sign of recognition from his son. Rick implored Morgan to shoot Duane and join him. Morgan feigned a gunshot inside the house. Instead of terminating Duane, he shot the chain tethering his son to the floor, leaving him free to roam.

ERIC

FIRST APPEARANCE: #68
LAST APPEARANCE: NA

STATUS: LIVING
FORMER OCCUPATION: UNKNOWN
CURRENT ROLE: SCOUT ASSISTANT
RELATIONS/ASSOCIATIONS: PARTNER TO AARON
POINT OF ORIGIN: INTRODUCED VIA AARON TO RICK IN ROUTE TO ALEXANDRIA
POINT OF DEPARTURE: UNDETERMINED

LIFE AMONG THEN:

The eyes and ears of the Alexandria scouting
team, charged with surveillance and evaluating new
recruits. Eric operated a long distance listening device
that allowed lead scout and partner Aaron to effectively
gauge the feasibility of potential new additions to their
community. He was also seldom visible, functioning as
what Aaron termed an 'insurance policy' or back-up in
the event that an evaluation went awry, requiring Eric
to kill a bad recruit.

Eric and Aaron's relationship extended beyond field
responsibilities, as they were also romantically partnered. They expressed deep affection for each other
upon returning to the safety of Alexandria. Their roles required them to quickly return to the decimated
world beyond the high walls of the safe-zone. However, on the following run, they attempted to bring
a nameless woman back to Alexandria. As the trio slept one evening on the return leg of their trip, Eric
awoke to find the woman stealing one of their prized horses.

He gently confronted her, trying to reason with her, but the woman turned on him suddenly, stabbing
him in the midsection and fleeing into the
darkness of the early morning with the horse.
Aaron placed Eric upon their remaining horse
and sprinted back to Alexandria where an
awaiting Doctor Cloyd was able to perform a
procedure to dress his wound and save Eric's
life.

NO WAY OUT:

After the breach of the walls of Alexandria
sent a deluge of walkers teeming through the
streets, Eric and Aaron sought refuge in their home. Watching from within, the partners
were inspired by Rick and Michonne's courage in fighting off the horde of zombies piling up in the
streets. Aaron was the first to move outside, but drawing from his partner's courage, Eric also
joined the fray and helped the other survivors wipe out the first massive wave of the undead.

EUGENE

FIRST APPEARANCE: #28
LAST APPEARANCE: #31

STATUS: DECEASED
FORMER OCCUPATION: UNKNOWN
CURRENT ROLE: WOODBURY RESIDENT, GOVERNOR'S MUSCLE, ARENA FIGHTER
RELATIONS/ASSOCIATIONS: GOVERNOR, DOC STEVENS, HAROLD, MICHONNE
POINT OF ORIGIN: THE NIGHT OF RICK'S CAPTURE, FOUGHT HAROLD AND LOST HIS TEETH
POINT OF DEPARTURE: DECAPITATED BY MICHONNE DURING AN ARENA MATCH

THE BEST DEFENSE:

Armed only with a baseball bat and remnant football gear, surrounded by chained walkers, Eugene performed as one of Woodbury's arena fighters. Under the bright lights of the outdoor stadium, Eugene engaged opponents in hand-to-hand combat; the object: avoid the bats and the biters and put on a good show to entertain his fellow Woodbury citizens.

On the eve of Rick's capture by the Governor, the fight went awry and a bat caught Eugene in the mouth, smashing out his teeth.

THIS SORROWFUL LIFE:

Angry with his condition, Eugene burst into Doc Stevens' operating room and confronted Harold, the arena fighter responsible for his toothless condition. Claiming the fights were always for show, an enraged Eugene stabbed Harold in the neck.

Eugene's next bout matched him against Michonne. The two combatants entered the arena - Eugene in his football shoulder-pads, bat in hand, Michonne in her signature poncho brandishing her blade. The former lawyer swift kicked Eugene in the genitals and with one fierce stroke from her blade, severed his head

EUGENE

FIRST APPEARANCE: #53
LAST APPEARANCE: NA

STATUS: LIVING
FORMER OCCUPATION: HIGH SCHOOL SCIENCE TEACHER
CURRENT ROLE: MEMBER OF ABRAHAM'S TRIO
RELATIONS/ASSOCIATIONS: ABRAHAM, ROSITA, RICK
POINT OF ORIGIN: INTRODUCED VIA ABRAHAM UPON MEETING RICK'S SURVIVORS
AT GREENE FAMILY FARM
POINT OF DEPARTURE: UNDETERMINED

HERE WE REMAIN:

"Doctor" Eugene Porter was one of a trio of travelers, including Abraham and Rosita, who crossed paths with Rick's survivors following the Governor's prison assault. Seeking refuge in Hershel Greene's empty farmhouse, Rick and the remaining survivors were surprised by the sudden appearance of Eugene's small band.

A tense standoff at gunpoint was defused when Eugene revealed that he had special knowledge of the cause of the zombie apocalypse. In fact, "Doctor" Porter claimed to be in radio contact with government officials in Washington, D.C., providing his field-based insight derived from studies of the undead during his journey to the capitol. When pressed, he was reluctant to reveal how he came by this information, but asserted himself to the group as a scientist versed in the study of biological weaponry, specifically, the weaponization of the human genome.

Eugene's claims yielded an uneasy truce between the factions. They cautiously merged, and soon began plotting a course for D.C.

LIFE AMONG THEM:

Eugene's appearance - his slovenly dress and mullet haircut - belied his scientific acumen. The truth of Eugene's background and mysterious radio communications were soon revealed when Rick physically challenged Eugene for the use of his radio.

Loosed from Rick's grasp, the two-way talkie crashed to the cement, the battery hatch jarred free from the casing. There at the feet of the stunned survivors was Eugene's radio, batteries not included...

...**Rick correctly surmised that the radio had never held batteries,** and that Eugene had never been in radio contact with Washington. Enraged, Abraham then beat a confession out of Eugene; he had been lying all along, not only about his background (he was merely a high school science teacher), but of his contact with government officials. He had misled the group and they were headed hopelessly into the unknown of Washington, D.C.

FATHER GABRIEL

FIRST APPEARANCE: #61
LAST APPEARANCE: NA

STATUS: LIVING
FORMER OCCUPATION: PRIEST
CURRENT ROLE: PRIEST
RELATIONS/ASSOCIATIONS: ABRAHAM, ROSITA, RICK
POINT OF ORIGIN: REVEALED HIMSELF TO RICK'S GROUP, LEADING THEM TO HIS CHURCH
POINT OF DEPARTURE: UNDETERMINED

FEAR THE HUNTERS:

No food, no companions and no weapons, save for the bible he carried, Father Gabriel Stokes made his presence known to Rick and his survivors with his arms raised in surrender, and an invitation to speak on the Lord. Alone in his church for quite some time, Father Gabriel abandoned the sanctuary after his food supplies were exhausted. On foot, he was able to avoid the undead by outrunning the occasional walker that crossed his path. While Abraham searched him for concealed weapons, Father Gabriel offered the group shelter in exchange for food, an offer Rick declined.

When the group was stalked and taunted by unseen assailants, Andrea blamed Father Gabriel, an idea which Rick quickly seized. On edge following the prison assault, Rick was of no mind to place his trust even in a man of God. He coerced Father Gabriel into divulging the truth, imploring any connection between him and the hunters as Andrea suspected.

Instead, Father Gabriel recounted the last several months of his life. With great shame and anguish, he revealed that at the outbreak of the undead apocalypse, he barred friends, neighbors, even members of his congregation, from entry to the church. They would surely eat all of his food, and he would starve. He had chosen self-preservation and remained sequestered safely in his church as the screams of the town's people mounted with great desperation. The impassioned confession moved Rick. He deemed Father Gabriel trustworthy, though Gabriel begged Rick to end his life, punishing him and in the process carrying out God's will for having allowed the deaths of so many.

TOO FAR GONE:

Having witnessed the murder of the hunters at the hands of Rick, Abraham, Michonne and Andrea, Father Gabriel unsuccessfully attempted to lobby Douglas Monroe to cast the group out of Alexandria. Douglas rebuffed his claims that the group was dangerous, even threatening Father Gabriel with expulsion himself should he continue to pursue the topic.

NO WAY OUT:

Huddled alone in his new church, Father Gabriel received a chance at redemption at the outset of the Alexandria crisis. He allowed Eugene and another resident access to his church:

GABE

FIRST APPEARANCE:
LAST APPEARANCE:

STATUS: **DECEASED**
FORMER OCCUPATION: **UNKNOWN**
CURRENT ROLE: **WOODBURY RESIDENT, THE GOVERNOR'S RIGHT HAND MAN**
RELATIONS/ASSOCIATIONS: **GOVERNOR, BRUCE, MICHONNE**
POINT OF ORIGIN: **ACCOMPANYING THE GOVERNOR AS HE GREETED RICK**
POINT OF DEPARTURE: **SHOT IN THE HEAD BY ANDREA DURING THE PRISON ASSAULT**

A member of the Governor's inner circle and a Woodbury resident, Gabe became second in command of Woodbury's forces following the death of Bruce Cooper, the Governor's personal armed guard.

Gabe was present and complicit in several key incidents involving the clash with the prison survivors, including the severing of Rick's hand and the Governor's rape of Michonne.

Loyal to a fault, Gabe appeared to follow the Governor's lead out of fear, lying to satisfy the Governor's wishes even when it came at a great cost. Having ambushed Michonne and Tyreese as they tracked the Governor back through the countryside following his first failed attack on the prison, Gabe falsely claimed he'd run down Michonne and 'blew her brains out,' producing her blade as evidence of his conquest.

Gabe's false bravado was exposed when Michonne turned up alive and attacked the Governor, nearly killing him with a semi-automatic. During the final assault on the prison, with grenades falling all around them, Gabe desperately tried to convince the Governor into another retreat. Claiming the Woodbury forces needed to regroup because they'd become unnerved by the opposition's tenacity, Gabe failed to persuade the Governor.

At the conclusion of his plea, Andrea's shot found Gabe's head, and his skull exploded in the Governor's face.

GLENN

FIRST APPEARANCE: #2
LAST APPEARANCE: NA

STATUS: LIVING
FORMER OCCUPATION: PIZZA DELIVERY, COLLEGE STUDENT
CURRENT ROLE: THIEF, SUPPLY RUNNER, SCOUT
RELATIONS/ASSOCIATIONS: MAGGIE, RICK, DALE, AMY, ANDREA, CAROL
POINT OF ORIGIN: RESCUED RICK FROM A SWARM OF WALKERS IN ATLANTA
POINT OF DEPARTURE: UNDETERMINED

DAYS GONE BYE:

Speed and agility, street savvy, and a talent for scavenging crucial supplies helped Glenn establish himself as a key member of the original survivors. In his former life, Glenn was a pizza delivery boy struggling with debt, on the verge of losing his apartment and car - a financial situation so severe that he considered crawling back to his parents for assistance, even though they had a fractured relationship. It was Glenn who discovered Rick and rescued him from certain death on the streets of Atlanta while on a supply run. He not only saved Rick's life (escorting him out of the city by jumping rooftops), he was also responsible for reuniting Rick with his family by bringing him back to camp. Glenn teamed with Rick on a return visit to Atlanta to retrieve guns and ammunition from a shop downtown.

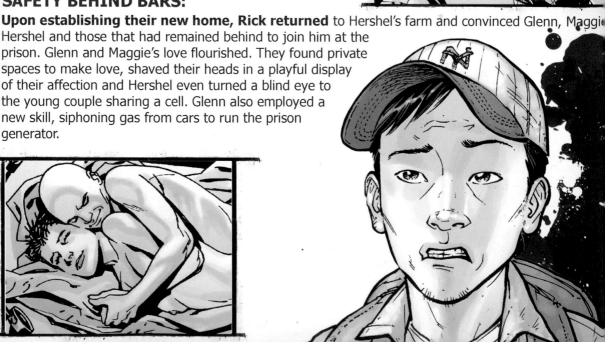

MILES BEHIND US:

At Hershel's Farm, Glenn would discover love upon meeting Hershel's daughter Maggie. Their early relationship was not without its difficulties, especially when Hershel discovered Maggie and Glenn in bed together. Yet, when Rick and the original survivors departed Hershel's Farm, Glenn confessed that he'd fallen in love and chose to remain behind.

SAFETY BEHIND BARS:

Upon establishing their new home, Rick returned to Hershel's farm and convinced Glenn, Maggie, Hershel and those that had remained behind to join him at the prison. Glenn and Maggie's love flourished. They found private spaces to make love, shaved their heads in a playful display of their affection and Hershel even turned a blind eye to the young couple sharing a cell. Glenn also employed a new skill, siphoning gas from cars to run the prison generator.

THE BEST DEFENSE:

After endless days of leisurely sex, Glenn and Maggie thoroughly explored the prison grounds and discovered the armory, fully stocked with firearms and full riot gear suits. Glenn accompanied Rick and Michonne to the site of a helicopter crash by hotwiring a car and driving them through the countryside. He was taken captive, however, outside the Woodbury security wall and imprisoned by the Governor, where he was intimidated by being made to listen to Michonne's torture.

THIS SORROWFUL LIFE:

Freed by Rick, Glenn returned to the prison only to find it overrun by walkers. He blacked out and was carried through to safety, where he fell into Maggie's awaiting arms. As they lay down in their cell, Glenn smelled smoke and Maggie told him that the fire was to incinerate the walkers. Bursting from their cell, Glenn ran out to the yard and began frantically searching the bodies of the undead until he located what he was searching for: a suitable wedding ring. Immediately upon returning from the yard, Glenn proposed marriage to Maggie, and she joyfully accepted.

THE CALM BEFORE - NO WAY OUT:

Hershel married Glenn and Maggie with his blessing and the group held a simple ceremony In the prison cafeteria. The couple then participated in a supply run during which Glenn obtained a crib and survived another near-death experience when he was shot by the Governor's scout team. Riot armor saved him from serious injury. The incident changed Glenn's desire to plan for a family and influenced his decision to leave the prison with Dale prior to the Governor's attack. Living in relative tranquility on Hershel's farm, the couple - now caring for an orphaned Sophia - reunited with Rick and several new faces. The reunion came sometime following the disastrous prison assault that claimed Maggie's father's life. Once again, they trusted Rick and joined with the group to travel to Washington, D.C., in hopes of salvation. Much to Maggie's growing fear, Glenn returned to his former role of supply runner on behalf of the Alexandria community. Paired with a new partner, Heath, Glenn confessed to experiencing an ever-growing sense of dread, that he could no longer envision a future for himself beyond the immediate moment. As if to prove this creeping notion true, Glenn was trapped outside the Alexandria security wall with Maggie and Sophia, surrounded by scores of countless walkers inside.

GOVERNOR

FIRST APPEARANCE: #27
LAST APPEARANCE: #48

STATUS: DECEASED
FORMER OCCUPATION: UNKNOWN
CURRENT ROLE: RULER OF WOODBURY
RELATIONS/ASSOCIATIONS: GABE, BRUCE, RICK, UNDEAD DAUGHTER, MICHONNE
POINT OF ORIGIN: WOODBURY ARENA
POINT OF DEPARTURE: SHOT IN THE HEAD BY FELLOW WOODBURY RESIDENT LILLY

THE BEST DEFENSE:

Self-proclaimed "Governor" of Woodbury, a four-block safe-zone populated by roughly 40 residents all under his unchallenged authority, Phillip was once a fair and even leader, making difficult decisions and doing everything within his power to ensure the safety of the growing community's residents. Somewhere along the way, Phillip became known only as the Governor, employing his sadistic methods of leadership to enthrall the populace of Woodbury with staged arena battles and threats of ruthless reprisals should they fail to heed his every command. When his scouts discovered Rick, Michonne and Glenn outside the security wall, they were escorted at gunpoint to meet the Governor. As the action in the arena kicked off, the Governor revealed several startling truths: Woodbury's defense was fueled by considerable firepower scavenged from the nearby National Guard Station, he was feeding the helicopter crash victims to the zombies in the arena, and he wanted Rick's trio to divulge the location of their 'camp' so he could pillage it for more supplies and victims. Horrified, Rick denied him the information, and the Governor responded in kind by chopping off his hand, imprisoning Glenn and raping Michonne repeatedly.

THIS SORROWFUL LIFE:

The Governor cunningly tricked Rick into revealing that his point of origin was indeed a prison. Healed from his forced amputation, Rick escaped with Martinez's help, in turn freeing Glenn and Michonne. Seeking revenge upon the Governor, Michonne caught him off guard in his apartment. She mutilated his genitals, removed his fingernails with pliers, drilled his shoulder with a screw gun

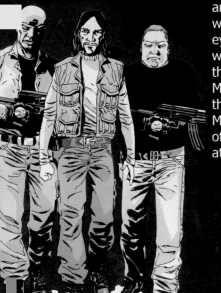

and using her sword, severed his arm, finally cauterizing the wound with a blow torch. When he regained consciousness, she popped his eyeball from the socket with a spoon. Before sneaking out a window, she nicked his femoral artery with her blade. Rick's band then fled Woodbury and returned to the prison. Almost immediately, Martinez attempted a return to Woodbury, but Rick ran him down in the R.V., killing him. The Governor's scouting party later discovered Martinez and used his death as propaganda to incite the residents of Woodbury to attack the prison.

Once the Governor healed, he set his sights upon the prison, mounting a massive assault. His envoy totaled eight vehicles and a tank. Clad in Rick's riot gear, eye patch covering his empty socket, the Governor ordered his forces to open fire. Andrea and Axel were winged by shots, but Andrea steadied herself. From high above the field in a guard tower, she systematically picked off the Governor's citizen soldiers with her sharpshooting, forcing his retreat.

Michonne and Tyreese went on the offensive, tracking the Governor back through the countryside. They were ambushed, and Tyreese was taken prisoner while Michonne escaped. With the upper hand, the Governor returned to the prison.

As Rick and the survivors looked on from behind the fences, the Governor revealed Tyreese bloodied and beaten. Punctuating the threat, he raised Michonne's blade over his head, threatening to behead Tyreese unless the gates were opened and all within surrendered. When the survivors did not respond to this ultimatum, the Governor slowly began severing Tyreese's head with a series of blows to the back of his neck, until it rolled freely to the grass, his lifeless body kicked from the back of the truck. Thoroughly frustrated that his merciless act did not bend the survivors to his will, the Governor returned to his awaiting soldiers. Michonne had been tracking the recent events and ambushed the group with a semi-automatic pointed at the back of the Governor's head. Gabe fired on Michonne, and the shot glanced off of the Governor's face, lacerating his cheek. Under heavy gunfire, Michonne grabbed her blade and fled.

Going for broke, the Governor initiated a final assault on the prison. They incurred heavy losses when Billy Greene began lobbing grenades from the guard station. Compounding matters, Andrea returned and killed Gabe, the Governor's lieutenant, with a headshot. Irrational, the Governor drove his tank through the gates of the prison and stormed the grounds.
With Rick's forces now in a terrified retreat, the Governor killed several of the opposition including Alice, Billy and Hershel. He then ordered Lilly to fire on Lori. When Lilly realized that her shot had killed both a mother and her infant daughter, she turned her rifle on the Governor and shot him through the head at close range. She then kicked his body into an onrushing horde of the undead, where his body was devoured.

GREG

FIRST APPEARANCE: #64
LAST APPEARANCE: #66

STATUS: **DECEASED**
FORMER OCCUPATION: **UNKNOWN**
CURRENT ROLE: **MEMBER OF THE HUNTER/CANNIBALS**
RELATIONS/ASSOCIATIONS: **ALBERT, CHRIS, DAVID, THERESA**
POINT OF ORIGIN: **INTRODUCED AS THE HOT-TEMPERED MEMBER OF THE GROUP**
POINT OF DEPARTURE: **KILLED BY ABRAHAM, ANDREA, MICHONNE & RICK**

FEAR THE HUNTERS:

One of a party of cannibalistic hunters that preyed upon solitary travelers or small groups of humans passing through the region. At first, like most survivors, Greg and his fellow hunters subsisted on scavenged stores and, on the rarest occasion, wild game.

Hunting animals ,however, proved exhaustive, yielding very little in return. Starving, with little recourse, it was decided that first the children of the group would be consumed. The remaining adults focused their efforts on other humans.

After Dale's abduction, the hunters amputated his lower leg, roasting it on a campfire spit. When Dale regained consciousness from the trauma, he revealed that he'd been bitten by a walker, rendering him 'tainted meat.' Sickened by Dale's condition, they soon returned Dale to the company of his own group- a fatal decision.

Rick, Michonne, Andrea, Abraham and Father Gabriel tracked the hunters back to their shelter in a housing tract not far from Father Gabriel's church. When confronted by Rick, Greg was eager to fire upon him but Chris ordered Greg to stand down. As the leader of the party, Chris told Rick of their tale, and the conditions that ultimately led them to cannibalism.

In retaliation, Rick signaled to Andrea to open fire from undercover. Her first shot clipped Greg on the ear, dropping him to the ground immediately, where Rick advised him to stay. After their firearms where taken by Abraham, Greg and every member of his party was executed and their remains burned in the campfire.

HEATH

FIRST APPEARANCE: #69
LAST APPEARANCE: NA

STATUS: LIVING
FORMER OCCUPATION: UNKNOWN
CURRENT ROLE: SUPPLY RUNNER/SCOUT
RELATIONS/ASSOCIATIONS: SCOTT, GLENN, DOCTOR CLOYD, DOUGLAS
POINT OF ORIGIN: INTRODUCED IN D.C. VIA AARON
POINT OF DEPARTURE: UNDETERMINED

LIFE AMONG THEM:

Returning to Alexandria with his newfound recruits, Aaron, Rick and his fellow survivors came rushing to aid of Heath and his severely wounded scouting partner, Scott. Using a flare to signal for assistance, Heath attracted Aaron's attention. With the aid of the new arrivals, Heath was able to fight his way through the teeming masses of zombies choking the streets of downtown Washington, D.C.

On a motorcycle, Heath's escape route was cut off but he got another reprieve when Tobin's security force arrived, guns blazing from the back of a pick-up truck. Safely back in Alexandria, Heath shared a private moment with Alexandria's leader Douglas Monroe. Heath unexpectedly incurred his wrath, however, when he expressed his concern over Rick's character. Douglas's violent reaction and swift physicality stunned Heath. It was clear the new survivor's arrival had unnerved the community.

TOO FAR GONE:

Heath kept a vigil over his fallen partner until Scott eventually passed away, due to complications from his broken leg. In doing so, Heath befriended and fell in love with Doctor Denise Cloyd. The two remained intimate, while Heath resumed his scouting duties, this time with a new partner, Glenn. Together, the fearless scouts scavenged medical supplies and other critical goods for the betterment of the community.

NO WAY OUT:

Heath also risked his life, along with Glenn and Spencer Monroe, carrying food and water to Andrea, who was stranded outside the walls of Alexandria in the city's clock tower as the community was overrun with walkers.

HERSHEL

FIRST APPEARANCE: #10
LAST APPEARANCE: #48

STATUS: DECEASED
FORMER OCCUPATION: **VETERINARIAN/FARMER**
CURRENT ROLE: **FARMER**
RELATIONS/ASSOCIATIONS: **FATHER TO ARNOLD, BILLY, LACEY, MAGGIE, RACHEL & SUSIE**
POINT OF ORIGIN: **REMOVED A BULLET FROM CARL'S SHOULDER AT HIS FARM**
POINT OF DEPARTURE: **SHOT IN THE HEAD BY GOVERNOR FOLLOWING PRISON ASSAULT**

MILES BEHIND US:

Hershel Greene's introduction to Rick and his fellow survivors came under less than auspicious conditions when his farmhand, Otis, accidentally shot Carl less than a mile from the farm. Hershel's veterinarian skills (honed from tending his livestock) allowed him to practice basic medicine. He successfully removed the bullet lodged in Carl's shoulder, and saved his life.

He accommodated the weary survivors and introduced them to his family: sons Arnold and Billy; daughters Lacey, Maggie, Rachel and Susie; as well as his live-in neighbors, Otis and Patricia. The first point of friction between Rick and Hershel flared up when Rick suggested the group stay in the barn. Hershel was quick to point out that the barn was used as a holding pen for walkers, comprised mainly of his neighbors that had turned and his son, Shawn. He had been sequestering the undead in the hopes of 'helping' them. Rick revealed that he preferred killing them. Despite Hershel's claims to the contrary, Rick believed them all to be permanently dead, never to be cured. Hershel bristled at this claim, and Tyreese intervened to calm the two men's tempers.

Eager to prove that capturing and containing walkers was a harmless exercise, Hershel restrained one that had roamed onto the property. When opening the door to his barn, he was pushed back onto his heels by those inside. He lost his balance, and the walkers rushed out to seize him. His eldest son, Arnold, jumped to his defense, but he was bitten by his undead brother, Shawn. In the resulting chaos, Lacey was devoured, and Hershel was forced to shoot all of his undead children and the remaining walkers.

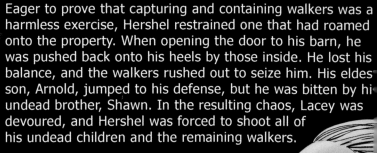

Hershel was a shaken man, and Rick had pushed him over the edge of his patience and goodwill following the burial of Arnold, Lacey and Shawn. Suggesting that the extra room in the house created by the recent deaths would be enough to accommodate Rick and his survivors, Hershel informed Rick that they were allowed to stay only through the remainder of Carl's convalescence. Lori angrily challenged Hershel. He nearly hit her, then he put a gun to Rick's head to stifle the argument. Once more, Rick and the survivors piled into the R.V. to face the unknown of the open road.

After the survivors settled in at the prison, Rick returned for Hershel and those who remained behind at the farm. Seeing the promise of a stronghold with living quarters and multiple fences to keep the walkers at bay, they naturally accepted Rick's invitation. Hershel prepared a garden on the grounds and mended his relationship with Rick. His coming to terms with the loss of his children was disrupted in horrific fashion when he found Rachel and Susie's beheaded bodies. Thomas revealed himself as the murderer when he attempted to attack Andrea. A man of deep religious faith, Hershel told Thomas that he forgave him for the atrocious act but agreed to watch him hang. Patricia tried to free Thomas before his execution but he turned on her. Her cries brought Tyreese running to her aid, armed and ready to kill. Maggie was standing behind Tyreese and she was not as liberal in her warning for Thomas to surrender; instead she shot him several times at close range. Later, Hershel watched silently as Thomas' body was pitched through the gates to the awaiting walkers.

Despite his broken heart, Hershel found solace and comfort in his surviving children. He gamely continued with his garden, plowing the grounds with the help of his son, Billy, and former inmate, Axel. He applied his medical skills to treat Carol after her attempted suicide and he also helped get the prison's power generator running. Despite their animosity, Hershel and Lori even became amicable in Rick's absence. More than anything, Hershel seemed at peace watching Maggie assert her independence through her growing relationship with Glenn. When he was approached by Glenn, who came bearing a ring, seeking Hershel's blessing for their marriage, Hershel wrapped Glenn in a fatherly embrace. With a small ceremony in the prison cafeteria, Hershel married Maggie and Glenn.

Hershel lost his life in the waning moments of the Governor's final attack on the prison. Billy was perched in the guard tower and Hershel was on the ground when the Governor rammed a tank through the fences. A hail of bullets and encroaching walkers meant that the only chance at survival was to run for the National Guard truck. Hershel gathered Billy from the tower and they attempted to time their escape. Axel and Patricia were shot dead in front of them as the father and son fled across the yard.

A shot pierced Billy's skull, and he fell lifeless from Hershel's grasp. Crushed, Hershel made no move to surrender or escape. He simply knelt at his dead son's side when the Governor's men found him. Angered by the presence of a survivor, the Governor placed his gun to Hershel's forehead. He raised his gaze to the sky, asked for God's forgiveness...then pleaded to be killed. The Governor obliged Hershel's final request.

HOLLY

FIRST APPEARANCE: #73
LAST APPEARANCE: NA

STATUS: LIVING
FORMER OCCUPATION: UNKNOWN
CURRENT ROLE: CONSTRUCTION CREW, ALEXANDRIA SECURITY WALL
RELATIONS/ASSOCIATIONS: ABRAHAM, TOBIN
POINT OF ORIGIN: INTRODUCED AS MEMBER OF TOBIN'S CREW
POINT OF DEPARTURE: UNDETERMINED

TOO FAR GONE:

The lone female member of Alexandria's construction team, tasked with expanding the security wall. During Abraham's first tour on the wall, Holly and several other members of the team were overrun by a swarm of walkers. Cut off from rescue, Tobin ordered the remaining crew members to retreat and form a 'phalanx,' abandoning Holly. Abraham took command, aggressively attacking the walkers, arming several members and rescuing Holly from certain death. After the melee concluded she turned on Tobin, striking him in the groin, as did Abraham, who called into question Tobin's suspect leadership skills. This was a gesture that Holly found especially gratifying.

NO WAY OUT:

Following Bruce's death, something more than gratification appeared to be at stake between Holly and Abraham. Holly privately confronted Abraham when he was forced to bludgeon Bruce after he had been mauled by walkers. She first challenged him, then thrust herself upon Abraham in apology. He rejected her embrace, not because he did not enjoy it, but for fear of being seen by the others, especially Rosita.

Holly survived the Alexandria catastrophe, fighting alongside Abraham and the others to clear the safe-zone of walkers, and appeared poised to help rebuild the community.

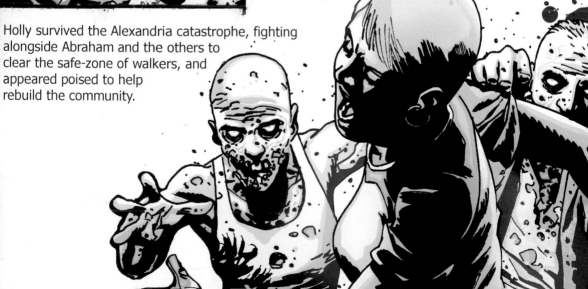

JESSIE

FIRST APPEARANCE: #72
LAST APPEARANCE: #83

STATUS: DECEASED
FORMER OCCUPATION: UNKNOWN
CURRENT ROLE: HOUSE WIFE
RELATIONS/ASSOCIATIONS: WIFE TO PETE, MOTHER OF RON
POINT OF ORIGIN: JESSIE MET RICK AT A PARTY AND THEN WHILE HE WAS ON PATROL
POINT OF DEPARTURE: DEVOURED BY ROAMERS FLEEING ALEXANDRIA

LIFE AMONG THEM:

Jessie first appeared beside her husband Pete and son Ron at the welcome party for the new Alexandria residents. Rick spied something curious about the young boy, a swollen and blackened eye.

TOO FAR GONE:

Rick later visited Jessie during a routine patrol, and she admitted that Pete had been beating both her and, more recently, Ron. When Pete came home and discovered Jessie and Rick, the conversation quickly ended and Rick excused himself. Later that evening, Rick returned, and when Pete answered the door Rick burst inside and assaulted him. The two men fought to a bloody standstill, ultimately crashing through the front window. When Rick failed to stand down on Douglas' orders, Michonne subdued him with a blow to the head.

The tormented Pete attempted to kill Rick with a knife. His glancing blow missed the mark, and instead slashed the throat of Douglas' wife, Regina. Spencer Monroe tackled Pete and as Regina died in his arms, Douglas ordered Rick to execute Pete.

NO WAY OUT:

Jessie appeared almost relieved by Pete's death. She was quick to forgive Rick, after he arrived to console her with an apology and some food for her and Ron. A bigger threat arose later, when Alexandria's security wall appeared on the brink of collapse. Jessie sought refuge with Carl and Rick. In the middle of night, she crawled into Rick's bed and kissed him. They seemed to show a growing love for one another that was ultimately short-lived. Jessie lost her life in the walker-infested streets of Alexandria. Rick tried to lead them outside the safe-zone's compromised wall, but Ron froze in fear and started pleading to go home. His cries attracted the attention of the walkers and the group was swarmed. Jessie clung to both of the boys. As she was swarmed, she refused to let go, trapping Carl. With no other recourse, Rick severed Jessie's hand with an axe, freeing Carl and leaving her behind to be devoured.

JIM

FIRST APPEARANCE: #2
LAST APPEARANCE: #6

STATUS: **DECEASED**
FORMER OCCUPATION: **MECHANIC**
CURRENT ROLE: **ORIGINAL CAMP MEMBER**
RELATIONS/ASSOCIATIONS: **N/A**
POINT OF ORIGIN: **ORIGINAL CAMP MEMBER**
POINT OF DEPARTURE: **BITTEN BY A ROAMER, JIM LOBBIED THE GROUP TO ABANDON HIM**

DAYS GONE BYE:

An original camp member, Jim was by far the most visibly impacted by the rise of the undead. He witnessed his former boss being attacked, the first man he'd seen bitten and turned. Jim claimed the transformation took only a matter of a couple of hours. That did not prepare Jim to watch his family get devoured, a story he could only bring himself to recount once and only to be retold to Rick by Glenn. Jim's wife, sister and her husband had acted as a human shield against the swarming walkers, protecting the five children they shared. Jim was only able to make his way to safety and escape Atlanta because the biters were busy eating his entire family.

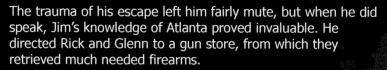

The trauma of his escape left him fairly mute, but when he did speak, Jim's knowledge of Atlanta proved invaluable. He directed Rick and Glenn to a gun store, from which they retrieved much needed firearms.

When the survivors suffered their first deadly attack by several roamers, Jim pulled his weight by defending the group. In the heat of the moment, he lost his senses, and resorted to hand-to-hand combat. Savagely striking a biter repeatedly with his gun, Jim's emotions for his family poured out. Shane finally calmed him, but after a moment of clarity, Jim discovered a large gouge on his forearm. He had been bitten. Over the course of a couple of days, longer than previously witnessed, Jim slowly succumbed to the effects of the undead. The survivors prepared to depart for Atlanta, and Jim pleaded with the group to leave him behind so that he might turn undead and reunite with his family once again.

They reluctantly honored his wishes, and left Jim propped against a tree on the outskirts of Atlanta.

JUDITH

FIRST APPEARANCE: #39
LAST APPEARANCE: #48

STATUS: DECEASED
FORMER OCCUPATION: N/A
CURRENT ROLE: N/A
RELATIONS/ASSOCIATIONS: RICK, LORI, SHANE, CARL, ALICE
POINT OF ORIGIN: INFANT DAUGHTER OF RICK AND LORI, SISTER TO CARL
POINT OF DEPARTURE: CRUSHED BENEATH LORI DURING THE GOVERNOR'S ATTACK

THE CALM BEFORE:

Judith Grimes was born as the survivors readied for the Governor's assault upon their prison sanctuary. Lori gave birth to baby 'Judy' with Rick and Alice's assistance. Although she was a source of joy, Judy's conception was the cause of great anguish, as she may have been conceived after Lori suspected Rick dead and had a brief affair with his former police partner Shane. Rick set aside his obvious pain, refusing to truly discuss the matter with Lori. He acknowledged the possibility that Judy might not be his daughter, yet still welcomed her into the family with all of his love.

MADE TO SUFFER:

Attempting to escape the Governor's deadly attack, Lori fled the prison with Judy cradled to her chest. A shot from a Woodbury soldier's rifle caught Lori in the midsection, exploded her abdomen, and sent her toppling over onto her infant daughter. Judy was crushed beneath Lori's lifeless body as Rick and Carl could do nothing more than run for the relative safety of the surrounding hillside.

JULIE

FIRST APPEARANCE: #7
LAST APPEARANCE: #15

STATUS: DECEASED
FORMER OCCUPATION: UNKNOWN
CURRENT ROLE: PARTNER TO CHRIS
RELATIONS/ASSOCIATIONS: DAUGHTER TO TYREESE, CHRIS
POINT OF ORIGIN: STUMBLED UPON THE SURVIVORS PRIOR TO THE PRISON
POINT OF DEPARTURE: SHOT BY HER PARTNER CHRIS IN A DOUBLE SUICIDE ATTEMPT

MILES BEHIND US:

Julie was traveling with her father, Tyreese, and her boyfriend Chris when they crossed paths with Rick's group. They joined the other survivors in Dale's R.V. The young couple contributed to the group's welfare by performing babysitting duties and other mundane tasks. At the Greene Family Farm, the group conducted firearm training after several members of the Greene family lost their lives to biters loosed from their barn. Tyreese allowed Julie and Chris to keep their guns, a decision that later proved deadly.

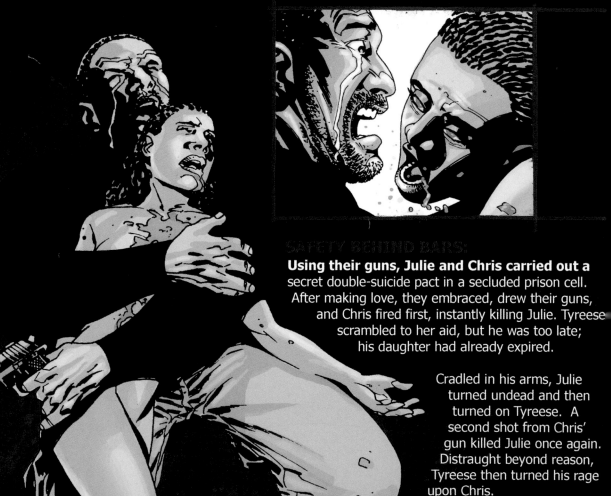

SAFETY BEHIND BARS:

Using their guns, Julie and Chris carried out a secret double-suicide pact in a secluded prison cell. After making love, they embraced, drew their guns, and Chris fired first, instantly killing Julie. Tyreese scrambled to her aid, but he was too late; his daughter had already expired.

Cradled in his arms, Julie turned undead and then turned on Tyreese. A second shot from Chris' gun killed Julie once again. Distraught beyond reason, Tyreese then turned his rage upon Chris.

LACEY

FIRST APPEARANCE: #10
LAST APPEARANCE: #11

STATUS: **DECEASED**
FORMER OCCUPATION: **FARM HAND**
CURRENT ROLE: **FARM HAND, ELDEST DAUGHTER IN THE GREENE FAMILY**
RELATIONS/ASSOCIATIONS: **DAUGHTER TO HERSHEL, SISTER TO ARNOLD, MAGGIE, BILLY, RACHEL & SUSIE**
POINT OF ORIGIN: **INTRODUCED AT THE GREENE FAMILY FARM**
POINT OF DEPARTURE: **DEVOURED BY BITERS HOUSED IN THE BARN**

MILES BEHIND US:

Hershel Greene's oldest daughter, Lacey, was like all of her fellow family members: a working hand on the farm. Hershel was a compassionate man of faith, and when he lost his son Shawn to a walker attack, he took to sequestering captured walkers in his barn in hopes of a cure. The Greene siblings, including Lacey, gathered about the barn as their father revealed how easy it was to subdue and contain a solitary biter. A surge of undead greeted Hershel at the barn door, sending him onto his back. The walkers poured forth and Hershel was defenseless. His son Arnold rushed to his father's aid, as did Lacey.

They were each quickly overwhelmed by walkers in the chaos. Lacey was devoured. Hershel was forced to shoot his undead family members, including Arnold, Shawn and last, Lacey.

LILLY

FIRST APPEARANCE: #48
LAST APPEARANCE: NA

STATUS: UNKNOWN (PRESUMED LIVING)
FORMER OCCUPATION: UNKNOWN
CURRENT ROLE: SOLDIER IN THE GOVERNOR'S ARMY
RELATIONS/ASSOCIATIONS: THE GOVERNOR, GABE, LORI, JUDITH
POINT OF ORIGIN: INTRODUCED DURING THE ASSAULT ON THE PRISON
POINT OF DEPARTURE: LEADING THE WOODBURY ARMY IN RETREAT FROM THE PRISON

MADE TO SUFFER:

As Carl, Rick, and Lori (who was cradling Judith) fled across
the prison yard in a desperate attempt to escape the Governor's
murderous rampage, Lilly was ordered to open fire upon the
defenseless Grimes family. Her lethal shot found Lori, the bullet
tearing through her midsection, killing her instantly. When Lilly
approached Lori's body, she discovered with great horror that her
shot had killed a mother and her infant daughter. Outraged by the
atrocity, Lilly trained her anger and gun on the Governor.

She clubbed her startled leader with the butt
of her rifle, and jammed the barrel in his mouth
as he fell to his knees. A wall of walkers struck
upon them, and the Governor seized the chance
to smack the rifle away, but they were
surrounded. Lilly recovered from the blow and
fired on the Governor.

At close range, the shot
exploded his skull.
She kicked his
dying body into the
throng of walkers,
and he was devoured.

Free of the Governor's merciless tyranny, Lilly called for a full retreat,
leading the charge against the ever encroaching swarm of biters
closing in upon the Woodbury army.

LORI

FIRST APPEARANCE:
LAST APPEARANCE:

STATUS: DECEASED
FORMER OCCUPATION: MOTHER/HOUSEWIFE
CURRENT ROLE: ORIGINAL CAMP MEMBER
RELATIONS/ASSOCIATIONS: WIFE TO RICK GRIMES, MOTHER TO CARL & BABY JUDITH
POINT OF ORIGIN: AT THE ORIGINAL CAMP OUTSIDE OF ATLANTA
POINT OF DEPARTURE: GUT SHOT BY LILLY DURING THE PRISON ASSAULT

DAYS GONE BYE - MILES BEHIND US:

Lori Grimes lived with the guilt of having left her husband Rick in a coma back home in Cynthiana, KY. Accompanied by Shane, Lori and her son Carl journeyed to Atlanta in hopes of reaching her parents. What they found was a city teeming with the dead. Overwhelmed with isolation, Lori turned to Shane for comfort. On the outskirts of the city, they made love before continuing on their way, joining with the original survivors. After several weeks, Rick miraculously appeared at the camp, escorted by Glenn. The Grimes family was reunited, and that meant Lori had a secret. She was able to fend off Shane's continued advances, even dismissing their one night together as a mistake. Having just been reunited with Rick, she loathed his return to Atlanta for guns and ammunition. As a mother, she vehemently protested when Rick gave then seven-year-old Carl a gun and trained him to use it.

SAFETY BEHIND BARS:

Lori could be outspoken and strong-willed.
She challenged Hershel when he told them to leave his farm, and she questioned Rick's judgment when he allowed the four inmates to remain at the prison. She also began to physically show her pregnancy. In Rick's absence, Lori and Dale falsely accused Dexter of the murder of Hershel's twin daughters, Rachel and Susie. Lori's decision to imprison Dexter led to his deep resentment and spurred Dexter and his partner Andrew to attempt a hostile takeover of the prison. This series of events cost Dexter his life when Rick later shot him in the head.

THE HEART'S DESIRE:

When Michonne arrived at the prison, Lori was one of the first survivors to befriend her. Though leery of the stranger, Lori engaged Michonne in conversation, getting her to share details of her life prior to the outbreak of the undead.

THE BEST DEFENSE:

A friendship with Carol continued to grow as Lori's pregnancy progressed. This took an unexpected turn when Carol suggested that they marry. Lori rejected Carol's advances on two occasions, opening an irreparable rift between the women.

THIS SORROWFUL LIFE:

When Rick returned from Woodbury with Alice, a medical assistant to Doc Stevens, Lori gained a measure of security for her pregnancy. Alice checked the baby's health and assured Lori and Rick that everything was progressing normally.

THE CALM BEFORE:

Just beneath the surface lingered the secret of Lori's night with Shane, and the nagging suspicion that the baby was his and not Rick's. Lori struggled with revealing this truth to her husband, and when she finally summoned the nerve, Rick cut her off, stating that he knew the truth of what Lori and Shane had done. He had suspected it all along, but it was far too painful to confront, too devastating to acknowledge. Lori managed an apology and Rick swore that though the truth of the baby's parentage would never be known, he would love it unconditionally. Soon thereafter, Lori gave birth to Judith, a baby girl the Grimes family welcomed into their hearts.

MADE TO SUFFER:

Judith's birth directly preceded the Governor's multiple assaults on the survivor's prison sanctuary. Many of the survivors lost their lives in the battles, and Lori and baby Judith were two particularly gruesome casualties. Lori, cradling baby Judith in her arms, tried to escape the prison with Rick and Carl leading the way. Lori was shot through the abdomen. The force of the bullet knocked her from her feet, and she toppled over onto Judith, who was still in her mother's arms. Lori and Judith perished together in the prison yard as Rick and Carl fled helplessly to the safety of the surrounding hillside.

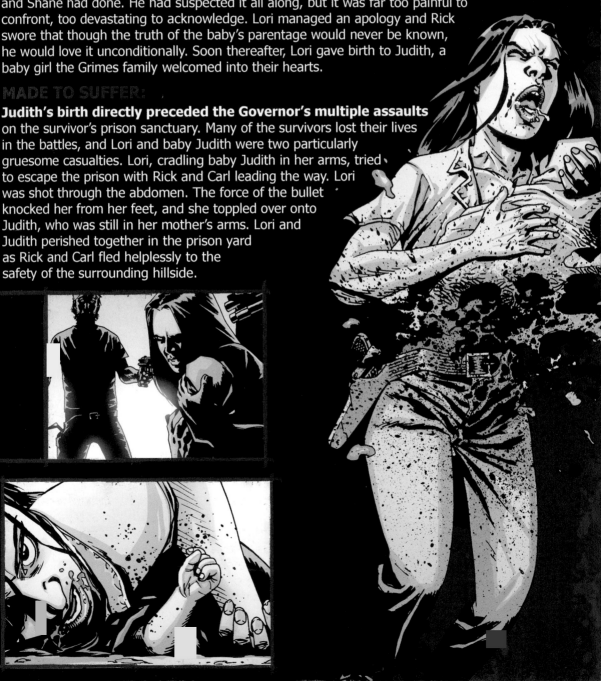

MAGGIE

FIRST APPEARANCE: #7
LAST APPEARANCE: #NA

STATUS: LIVING
FORMER OCCUPATION: FARM HAND
CURRENT ROLE: WIFE TO GLENN
RELATIONS/ASSOCIATIONS: DAUGHTER OF HERSHEL, SISTER OF LACEY, ARNOLD, BILLY, RACHEL & SUSIE
POINT OF ORIGIN: INTRODUCED AT THE GREENE FAMILY FARM
POINT OF DEPARTURE: UNDETERMINED

MILES BEHIND US:

Maggie Greene was introduced by Hershel as his middle daughter upon the survivors' arrival at his farm. At dinner that evening, Maggie noticed Glenn staring longingly at Carol, then coupled with Tyreese. On the porch afterwards, she found Glenn sitting alone, and questioned him about his staring; Glenn admitted to being lonely. She bluntly offered him sex, and Glenn very readily accepted.

SAFETY BEHIND BARS:

When Hershel kicked the survivors out of his home, Glenn chose to remain behind with Maggie, but when Rick returned days later with news of a prison suitable for long-term habitation, the young couple accepted his offer, and relocated. Maggie was happy to assert her independence from Hershel since he strongly objected to her and Glenn's 'sinful' relationship.

During this period, Maggie lost her twin sisters Rachel and Susie when Thomas, a former inmate, decapitated them both. Having watched Arnold and Lacey get devoured by walkers, Maggie had hardened around the edges. When the opportunity presented itself, she took her revenge and shot Thomas several times, killing him.

THE BEST DEFENSE:

At every opportunity Maggie and Glenn explored the prison, finding secluded areas for lovemaking, and their investigative endeavors led them to a storeroom filled with riot gear, armor and guns - crucial protection in defending themselves against the undead.

THIS SORROWFUL LIFE:

What began as merely a relationship of sexual convenience soon evolved, and Maggie accepted Glenn's marriage proposal after he returned from his extended capture in Woodbury. Having received Hershel's blessing, Maggie and Glenn married with a simple ceremony in the prison cafeteria presided over by her father, a final moment of family harmony and reconciliation before Hershel and Maggie's brother Billy lost their lives during the Governor's assault on the prison.

MADE TO SUFFER - HERE WE REMAIN:
Maggie did not witness her father and brother's deaths since she had chosen to abandon the prison for the relative safety of her old home. The looming threat of the Governor's return inspired Maggie and Glenn to accept Dale and Andrea's offer to leave. Since Sophia had been orphaned after Carol's death, Maggie and Glenn assumed care of her, and they became her surrogate parents.

Well after the deadly clash at the prison, Maggie and Glenn discovered Rick and Michonne sitting in the roadway while Carl slept in the vehicle's backseat. Rick grimly explained the outcome of the prison fight - news that left Maggie mourning the loss of Hershel and Billy.

When new survivors arrived at the farm, allegedly possessing information of salvation awaiting them in Washington, D.C., Maggie demanded that she and Glenn join them. Embittered by her father and brother's deaths, she wanted nothing more than to leave her family home and forget her former life.

WHAT WE BECOME - TOO FAR GONE:
Maggie showed an emotional fragility as the rigors of the journey mounted. Her tenuous hold on her emotions broke on the heels of the deaths of twins Ben and Billy. One evening, as the survivors struggled to clear the roadway of a wrecked vehicle, Maggie crept into the woods. Glenn assumed she had simply taken the opportunity to privately relieve herself, but he was shocked to find that Maggie had hung herself from a tree. He freed her from the crudely fashioned noose, and attempted to resuscitate her lifeless body. Abraham yanked Glenn from her and readied a head shot, expecting Maggie to reanimate as the undead at any moment. Rick stepped in and pointed a gun to his temple when Abraham did not heed Glenn's plea to continue. Maggie's desperate act proved unsuccessful, when she heaved in a great rasping breath and bolted upright, alive.

Sometime later, Maggie admitted to Glenn that the combination of not being able to conceive a child and her family's deaths took her to a 'dark place.' Hanging from the rope, she'd realized there was no heaven, no salvation, and no greater place beyond this life. She told Glenn, genuinely, that he was her reason for living because he made this life worthwhile.

NO WAY OUT:
Maggie and Glenn settled in Alexandria, and much to Maggie's objection, Glenn resumed his role as a scout. After the fall of the security wall, Glenn was trapped outside the 'safe-zone' while Maggie chose to remain behind with Sophia instead of following Rick's attempted escape through the undead. Her decision proved prescient. Several survivors were killed or wounded while Maggie and Sophia remained unharmed.

MARAUDERS

FIRST APPEARANCE: #57
LAST APPEARANCE: #57

STATUS: **DECEASED**
FORMER OCCUPATION: **UNKNOWN**
CURRENT ROLE: **A TRIO OF MARAUDERS**
RELATIONS/ASSOCIATIONS: **ABRAHAM, CARL, RICK,**
POINT OF ORIGIN: **AMBUSHED RICK, CARL AND ABRAHAM DURING A TRIP TO RICK'S HOME**
POINT OF DEPARTURE: **MURDERED BY RICK IN HAND-TO-HAND COMBAT**

WHAT WE BECOME:

A trio of marauders ambushed Rick, Carl and Abraham on the road to Cynthiana, KY, as they returned to visit Morgan and Duane. At gunpoint, they attempted to pillage their supplies and steal their transportation. When Rick and Abraham fought back, they changed tactics, taking Carl at knife point. One of the three tried to rape Carl. Seeing his son on the brink of being sexually molested enraged Rick and he furiously fought back.

Using only his mouth, Rick ripped a hunk of flesh from his assailant's neck, effectively incapacitating the man. Abraham used the distraction to arm himself and shoot the man holding him captive. The remaining marauder, the one who pinned Carl beneath him and taunted Rick moments before the turn in fortune, pleaded for mercy, but Rick, still seething with rage, used one of their own hunting knives to kill him while Abraham consoled a shaken Carl.

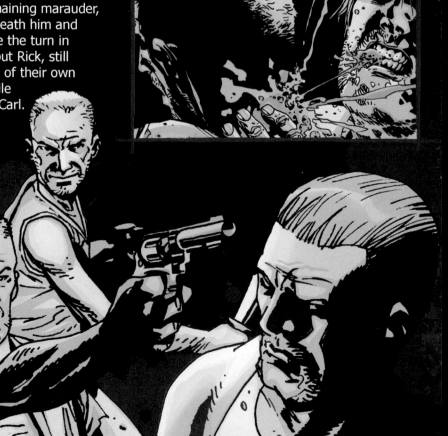

MARTINEZ

FIRST APPEARANCE: #27
LAST APPEARANCE: #43

STATUS: **DECEASED**
FORMER OCCUPATION: **GYM TEACHER**
CURRENT ROLE: **SECURITY GUARD/MEMBER OF THE GOVERNOR'S INNER CIRCLE**
RELATIONS/ASSOCIATIONS: **THE GOVERNOR, RICK, DOC STEVENS, ALICE**
POINT OF ORIGIN: **SPOTTED RICK, GLENN AND MICHONNE AT THE WOODBURY WALL**
POINT OF DEPARTURE: **RUN DOWN BY RICK WITH THE R.V. THEN STRANGLED TO DEATH**

THE BEST DEFENSE:

A guard on the Woodbury security wall, Martinez discovered Rick, Michonne and Glenn outside the wall and escorted the trio to their fateful meeting with the Governor. A former gym teacher, Martinez was a single man, estranged from his parents, alone in the world with nothing to lose. All of that changed as the school where he taught was overrun. He remained haunted by memories of the crying children, calling out for their mothers as the undead overwhelmed the police and firemen guarding the 'safe haven' of the school. He fled as the walkers devoured the children. This decision was a source of gnawing regret for Martinez.

THIS SORROWFUL LIFE:

These experiences seemed lost upon him, when he was dispatched by the Governor to accompany Rick and his fellow survivors back to the prison. Martinez was tasked with facilitating their escape, then returning to Woodbury. If successful, doing so would have revealed the survivors' location - information Martinez appeared destined to carry back to the Governor, until Rick ran him down with Dale's R.V. The collision left Martinez crippled. In his final moments, Rick choked a confession out of him. He contended that he never intended to bring the Governor back to the prison. Instead, he wished to escort the women and children of Woodbury to the safety of the prison, a claim Rick did not appear to believe. Martinez expired, and Rick left his body in the field as a few roamers closed in from a distance. The Governor's men later discovered Martinez and severed his head, which the Governor used to incite the citizens of Woodbury to attack the prison.

MICHONNE

FIRST APPEARANCE: #19
LAST APPEARANCE: #NA

STATUS: LIVING
FORMER OCCUPATION: ATTORNEY, MOTHER
CURRENT ROLE: CONSTABLE OF ALEXANDRIA
RELATIONS/ASSOCIATIONS: TYREESE, RICK, CARL, MORGAN, THE GOVERNOR
POINT OF ORIGIN: APPEARED OUTSIDE THE PRISON, TWO ZOMBIES CHAINED TO HER SIDES
POINT OF DEPARTURE: UNDETERMINED

THE HEART'S DESIRE:

Michonne appeared quite literally from nowhere, some distance from the prison. Otis was under attack by walkers, and Michonne decapitated them all with her blade. Clad in a hooded poncho, brandishing a long katana sword with two partially dismembered biters chained to her sides, Michonne requested that Otis repay her by helping her gain entry to the prison. Upon greeting Rick, she sliced the heads from each of her undead escorts, relinquished her weapon, and joined the survivors inside their stronghold. Upon settling into her new surroundings, Michonne recognized Tyreese as a former Atlanta Falcons football player. They formed an immediate bond, one that drove a wedge between Tyreese and Carol when she later witnessed them together in the gym.

Somewhat of an enigma, Michonne was not very forthcoming. Andrea found her carrying on a conversation with herself while alone in her cell, though later Lori was able to gain some insight into her past. Michonne revealed that she had had two daughters, parents, two sisters, a brother, a boyfriend (one of the undead chained to her side), an ex-husband, and even a mortgage, but all had been lost when the dead rose and claimed their lives.

Her aggressive pursuit of Tyreese triggered Carol's suicide attempt and touched off a bloody brawl between Rick and Tyreese when he discovered the new lovers in an embrace.

THE BEST DEFENSE:

When a helicopter crashed in close proximity to the prison, Michonne accompanied Rick and Glenn on a quest to locate it. Following the tracks of the supposed survivors led the trio to the walls of Woodbury. Michonne, Rick and Glenn were taken captive by the Governor. When he severed Rick's hand to force information out of him, Michonne attacked him, biting off the Governor's ear. She was imprisoned, raped and tortured.

THIS SORROWFUL LIFE:

Michonne was freed by Rick and Woodbury security guard Martinez. Instead of returning to the prison, she chose to remain behind. She burst into the Governor's apartment where he was feeding his undead daughter, and quickly overwhelmed him. Michonne exacted every measure of revenge for all that she had suffered by his han She mutilated his body - using her sword, pliers, a power drill, a blowtorch and a spoon to remove his eye from the socket. Before sneaking out a window, she nicked his femoral artery with her blade.

THE CALM BEFORE - MADE TO SUFFER:

Returning to the prison, Michonne sought comfort in Tyreese's arms. In a rare moment of unguarded emotion, she climbed into his bed and cried herself to sleep in his embrace. Following the Governor's failed attack on the prison, Michonne convinced Tyreese that together they could sneak into Woodbury and kill several unsuspecting members of their army. Michonne reasoned this would weaken the Governor's ranks and stifle his desire to attack the prison once again. Their plan failed when Michonne and Tyreese stumbled upon the Governor's scouts long before reaching Woodbury. Tyreese was captured while Michonne escaped, but not before losing her blade.

The Governor used Michonne's sword to decapitate Tyreese. Tracking the events from the cover of the woods surrounding the prison, Michonne mounted another attack, this time against the Governor. Her ambush proved unsuccessful, but she managed to retrieve her weapon. The Governor subsequently overwhelmed those survivors left defending the prison.

HERE WE REMAIN:

Alone once again, Michonne returned to the prison to survey the scene. She found Tyreese, hi severed head reanimated, lying in the tall grass. A single stroke of her blade plunged through his temple and ended Tyreese. Using the tracks left by Rick and Carl, Michonne began her journey to reunite with the remaining survivors. She discovered Carl in an old El Camino parked in the middle of road just as he was about to be devoured by a walker. She saved his life with her blade and he joyfully jumped into her arms. She joined Rick and Carl as they roamed the countryside, fruitlessly trying to locate Hershel's farm. Michonne learned the deadly fate of several survivors, playing the role of confidant to Rick, who repeated second-guessed decisions he had made, which cost people their lives. Michonne brought him around with some stern advice to move forward and locate Hershel's farm. Never particularly close, their bond deepened when Rick found Michonne talking to herself as Andrea had after Michonne had first arrived at the prison. She confessed that her conversations were with her dead boyfriend. Her fear of Rick's judgment was instantly dissipated when Rick revealed the old phone he used to talk with Lori. 'Crazy,' was how Michonne termed their condition, which they agreed to keep to themselves.

WHAT WE BECOME:

The trio's ranks grew after reuniting with old friends and welcoming new survivors. Michonne continued to work up Rick's confidence, being a sounding board for his ideas and reassuring him when he took action.

FEAR THE HUNTERS:

She entrusted Rick enough to ask his opinion of Morgan, hinting that she had feelings for him since he'd joined their group. Any possible chance for romance was tabled when the group found that they were being stalked by cannibals. After Rick tracked the 'hunters' to their lodging, Michonne helped kill and burn the entire group.

LIFE AMONG THEM:

On the road to Washington, D.C., the survivors were escorted to a 'safe-zone' in the nearby suburb of Alexandria. Michonne settled into the community much like her fellow survivors. In her assigned home, she hung her blade over a mantle, retiring her weapon. She tried to assimilate, but a certain nagging uneasiness pervaded her thoughts. She

was uncomfortable at the community welcome party while established residents blathered on about mundane banalities. Her relationship with Morgan slowly began to form as they recognized their mutual disdain for seemingly trivial conversations and diversions.

TOO FAR GONE:

Michonne was assigned duty as Rick's partner, performing routine patrols of the community as Alexandria's constable. To her disappointment, Morgan waffled about their relationship, alternately making love with Michonne then fleeing her bed afterwards, ridden with guilt and self-loathing. Each time Morgan broke down, Michonne welcomed him back. On one occasion, she bluntly chastised Morgan for his feelings, a moment of anger she regretted. Moreover, Michonne had to step in and rescue Rick from his own self-destructive behavior when he overzealously pursued bringing justice to bear upon Pete for having beaten his wife and son. When it appeared Rick had spiraled completely out of control, Michonne assaulted him and ordered Rick to 'get his shit together.'

NO WAY OUT:

Her fortitude remained unparalleled in the face of disaster and death. Morgan was lost when Alexandria was overrun by walkers. He was bitten, and even Michonne's quick amputation of his arm could not save his life.

As Morgan expired from his wounds, Michonne confessed her love for him. She used her blade to ensure he would not rise from the dead, then joined Rick as he led an escape. When their attempt failed, she remained in the streets of Alexandria, fighting by Rick's side for their lives. Their courage inspired others to join them, and the survivors staved off their deadliest threat to date.

MIKEY

FIRST APPEARANCE: #71
LAST APPEARANCE: #NA

STATUS: LIVING
FORMER OCCUPATION: N/A
CURRENT ROLE: ALEXANDRIA RESIDENT
RELATIONS/ASSOCIATIONS: SON TO NICHOLAS
POINT OF ORIGIN: CHALLENGED CARL FOR THE RIGHT TO SEE HIS GUN
POINT OF DEPARTURE: UNDETERMINED

LIFE AMONG THEM:

When Mikey asked Carl to see his gun, Carl refused.
Angered by the newcomer's refusal to share, Mikey pushed
Carl out of frustration. Trained to respect the use of his gun,
Carl shoved Mikey to the ground. Rick intervened, and gently
chastised Carl. Carl apologized to Mikey, offering him a hand
up, but the boy remained spiteful.

Embarrassed, Mikey threatened
to tell his father that Carl had
attacked him, even though he
had provoked Carl by asking to
see his gun, then heightened the
confrontation by pushing him first.

After Mikey stormed off, Rick praised Carl for properly protecting
his firearm, but warned him that he could not do so by harming the
other children.

Mikey then returned with his father, Nicholas, who angrily and falsely
accused Carl of being the aggressor in the altercation.

MORGAN

FIRST APPEARANCE: #1
LAST APPEARANCE: #83

STATUS: DECEASED
FORMER OCCUPATION: UNKNOWN
CURRENT ROLE: FATHER TO DUANE
RELATIONS/ASSOCIATIONS: FATHER TO DUANE, RICK, MICHONNE
POINT OF ORIGIN: NURSED RICK BACK TO HEALTH AFTER HE WAS STRUCK BY A SHOVEL
POINT OF DEPARTURE: DIED FOLLOWING A WALKER BITE AND AMPUTATION

DAYS GONE BYE:

Morgan Jones and his son Duane were Rick's first human contact after he returned home from the hospital in hopes of finding his family at their home. What Rick found was Duane's shovel, when the boy mistakenly thought he was a walker, and hammered him in the back of the head. Morgan moved Rick's unconscious body into their home, and after Rick regained consciousness, they shared dinner and a conversation. With the little information he had, Morgan tried to illustrate for Rick how the undead had risen, and how society had crumbled. Morgan and Duane accompanied Rick to the Cynthiana Police Department, where he outfitted Morgan with rifles and bullets before he departed for Atlanta in search of Carl and Lori.

WHAT WE BECOME:

Well over a year later, Rick returned to Cynthiana and discovered an emaciated and distraught Morgan still encamped in his old neighbor's home. History repeated itself when Rick was greeted yet again by a shovel, but this time it was Morgan's. Rick shielded himself against another blow as the faint glimmer of recognition sparked in Morgan's wild eyes. Morgan tearfully revealed Duane, undead, and described how he'd been swarmed and bitten some three months prior. Shackled to the floor by a chain, Morgan admitted to killing dogs and four men, then feeding their remains to Duane. He hoped that somehow his boy would show some recognition and respond to his father as he had before he turned. Rick convinced his old friend to join him on the road to Washington, D.C. Morgan took Rick's gun and feigned killing Duane. Instead, he shot the chain that tethered Duane to the floor, allowing him to roam free.

Formerly affable and good natured for all appearances, Morgan was a broken man. He was taciturn and withdrawn on the journey to Washington D.C. Once inside the walls of Alexandria, having survived the largest walker herd witnessed by the survivors, Morgan reached out to Carl, whom he viewed as a surrogate for Duane.

Morgan and Michonne began to form a tenuous bond. During a welcome party for the new arrivals, Morgan and Michonne discovered that each could not stomach the false frivolity of the Alexandria residents, and departed early. The two spent the night together, but Morgan awoke the next morning regretful and guilty for having had the pleasure of Michonne's company only a little over a year since losing his wife. His sentiment seemed to wound Michonne.

Morgan and Michonne reconciled, but their relationship suffered as Morgan would recall his wife wrestle with his guilt, and attempt to rationalize his happiness as being deserved. Their struggle as a couple soon ended when the Alexandria security wall fractured, allowing walkers into the 'safe-zon' Defending the community against the undead, Morgan was bitten severely on the arm. Without the aid of a medic, Rick ordered Michonne to amputate his arm in order to stop him from turning.

Morgan teetered on the edge of deatl even after Doctor Cloyd dressed his shoulder. Afflicted with a high fever, he ducked in and out of lucidity, and even mistakenly referred to Carl as his son, Duane.

Michonne relieved Carl of his guard duty where he had kept a close watch over Morgan. She admitted how mucl she cared for him, and asked Morgan forgiveness for her sometimes harsh behavior towards him.

Her heartfelt apology came too late; Morgan had quietly passed away. Michonne then used her blade to ensure that Morgan would never return.

NICHOLAS

FIRST APPEARANCE: #71
LAST APPEARANCE: #NA

STATUS: LIVING
FORMER OCCUPATION: UNKNOWN
CURRENT ROLE: ALEXANDRIA RESIDENT
RELATIONS/ASSOCIATIONS: FATHER TO MIKEY
POINT OF ORIGIN: ANGRILY CONFRONTED RICK AFTER MIKEY AND CARL FOUGHT
POINT OF DEPARTURE: UNDETERMINED

LIFE AMONG THEM:

Nicholas was Mikey's father, the young boy who demanded to see Carl's gun upon his arrival at Alexandria. When Carl refused Mikey's request, he pushed Carl, who retaliated in kind by shoving Mikey to the ground. Refusing Carl's apology, Mikey told his father, and Nicholas angrily confronted Rick.

Rick defused the situation but Nicholas truly took exception to the fact that Carl was toting a gun. His objection to the new arrivals being armed provoked Douglas to request that all weapons, including Carl's gun, be surrendered to their custody, should Rick's party choose to stay. At a welcome party for the new arrivals, Nicholas apologized to Rick for the confrontation, a gesture Rick regarded with genuine appreciation.

OLIVIA

FIRST APPEARANCE: #70
LAST APPEARANCE: NA

STATUS: LIVING
FORMER OCCUPATION: UNKNOWN
CURRENT ROLE: ALEXANDRIA COLONY RESIDENT, MUNITIONS GAURD, HAIR CUTTER
RELATIONS/ASSOCIATIONS: RICK, TOBIN, GLENN
POINT OF ORIGIN: INTRODUCED TO RICK WHEN CUTTING HIS HAIR
POINT OF DEPARTURE: UNDETERMINED

LIFE AMONG THEM:

The openly friendly Olivia was a font of information, as well as the gate-keeper for the Alexandria armory and food stores. Olivia made Rick's acquaintance after Douglas dispatched her with a policeman's uniform for Rick to wear in his new role.

She also gave him a much-needed haircut, along with valuable insight into Alexandria's history.

While cutting his hair, Olivia told Rick about the founding of the safe-zone by Alexander Davidson. After the location wa established, construction of the security wall commenced under Davidson's direction. Later, Douglas Monroe arrived and assumed leadership of Alexandria.

She explained to Rick that early life in the community had r run smoothly. The residents relied upon on a glitch-plagued solar power grid that caused several homes to go without power, and they lived with intermittent hot water.

Rick laughed off Olivia's stories, comparing his existence outside the walls of Alexandria against the abundance of creature comforts provided within the safe-zone.

Olivia had the last word, telling Rick that within a couple of weeks, he too would find even the smallest trifling inconvenience worthy of complaint.

OTIS

FIRST APPEARANCE: #9
LAST APPEARANCE: #30

STATUS: **DECEASED**
FORMER OCCUPATION: **FARM HAND**
CURRENT ROLE: **FARM HAND**
RELATIONS/ASSOCIATIONS: **HERSHEL GREENE & FAMILY, PATRICIA**
POINT OF ORIGIN: **INTRODUCED AT THE GREENE FAMILY FARM AS A NEIGHBOOR AND FRIEND**
POINT OF DEPARTURE: **SHOT BY RICK AFTER TURNING UNDEAD**

MILES BEHIND US:

Out foraging the surrounding countryside, Otis shot Carl through the shoulder, mistaking him for a walker, and in doing so, incurred Rick's full fury. Panicked and remorseful, Otis led them to Hershel Greene's farm. Carl lived, and the survivors enjoyed their first shelter since breaking camp.

With his girlfriend Patricia, Otis struck out for Atlanta during the undead outbreak, but got stalled at Wiltshire Estates. They returned, took up residence with Hershel and began assisting with the farm.

THE HEART'S DESIRE:

Otis remained there to tend the livestock even after the Greene family relocated to the prison. He was overrun by walkers on a routine supply run, but it was luck that Michonne appeared from nowhere and came to his aid. She saved his life and asked for admittance to the prison in return. Otis and Michonne arrived at the end of a fatal uprising staged by Dexter, which was cut short by a walker invasion of the prison grounds. The incidents convinced Otis that he should join the other survivors. He became estranged from Patricia after he learned that she had aided in Dexter's failed coup, then later tried to free Thomas after he murdered Hershel's twins. Otis forgave Patricia just shortly before his death.

THE BEST DEFENSE:

Assisting with the prison gates upon Tyreese's return from a scouting mission, Otis was lost in the tide of undead crashing against the barriers. In the scramble to get the R.V. back through gates - and get Tyreese to safety - no one noticed Otis had gone missing.

THIS SORROWFUL LIFE:

When Rick returned from Woodbury, he stepped upon Otis's disemboweled body while fending off yet another round of biters. Clawing meekly at Rick with the thirst of the undead, Rick quickly terminated Otis's life with a bullet through his head.

PATRICIA

FIRST APPEARANCE:
LAST APPEARANCE:

STATUS: DECEASED
FORMER OCCUPATION: FARM HAND
CURRENT ROLE: FARM HAND
RELATIONS/ASSOCIATIONS: THE GREENE FAMILY, THOMAS, DEXTER, OTIS, AXEL
POINT OF ORIGIN: INTRODUCED AT THE GREENE FAMILY FARM
POINT OF DEPARTURE: SHOT IN THE HEAD DURING THE PRISON ASSAULT

SAFETY BEHIND BARS:

Patricia was accompanying her boyfriend Otis to Atlanta when the city was overrun by the undead. They took refuge in Wiltshire Estates, but turned back soon thereafter. They remained at Hershel Greene's farm, but Patricia left when Rick's survivors located the prison. A series of poor decisions led Patricia to be ostracized by the survivors. She first tried to free Thomas from captivity after he was slated for execution for the murder of Rachel and Susie. Thomas turned on Patricia and nearly choked her to death.

THE HEART'S DESIRE:

With Rick and the other survivors preoccupied with Thomas's fate, Patricia returned inside the prison to join Dexter and Andrew as they armed themselves in preparation to overthrow Rick and his fellow survivors. When Dexter revealed his desire to kill Rick, Patricia pleaded with him to keep his word and only force them to leave.

THE BEST DEFENSE - THE CALM BEFORE:

After Rick killed Dexter and Otis returned to the prison, Patricia found herself a pariah. Shortly before his death, Otis asked for Patricia's friendship - a request she begrudgingly granted. Only later did Patricia find some acceptance from the group: she acknowledged to Hershel her deep sense of loss for all those that died, assisted in the garden and offered to help Lori care for Carl and Judith.

MADE TO SUFFER:

When Patricia and the lone remaining former inmate Axel formed an intimate bond, it seemed as if Patricia might have finally found solace in a far too unforgiving world. The Governor's raid upon the prison cut their growing relationship short. Axel was shot dead in front of her, and then Patricia was shot through the face trying to lead Billy and Hershel across the prison yard to safety.

PETE

FIRST APPEARANCE:
LAST APPEARANCE:

STATUS: **DECEASED**
FORMER OCCUPATION: **UNKNOWN**
CURRENT ROLE: **FATHER AND HUSBAND, ALEXANDRIA COLONY RESIDENT**
RELATIONS/ASSOCIATIONS: **HUSBAND TO JESSIE, FATHER TO RON**
POINT OF ORIGIN: **DISCOVERED SLEEPING ON THE PORCH DURING RICK'S PATROL**
POINT OF DEPARTURE: **SHOT IN THE HEAD BY RICK**

TOO FAR GONE:

Pete was awakened on his porch one morning by Rick, who was making the rounds on his daily patrol. Rick introduced himself, and recalled Pete from the party the evening prior. Pete had arrived with his wife Jessie and their son, Ron, whom Rick had spotted playing football in the street upon his arrival at Alexandria days before. Rick noted Ron's blackened eye. As Alexandria's new constable, Rick's suspicion led him to investigate the matter. When he confronted Ron, he was hesitant to offer a response, blaming his condition on a stray football. Pete shrugged off Rick's questioning, and identified the wound as the result of typical boyhood exuberance. Pete also explained that, on occasion, he slept on the porch after he and Jessie fought, as if this behavior was nothing out of the ordinary.

Later that afternoon Pete returned from his duties to find Rick talking with Jessie, and tensions rose. That evening, Pete opened his door to a loud pounding. Rick had returned. Pete angrily confronted him, and a fist fight ensued. The altercation carried the two men through the living room window. Douglas and Michonne stopped the brawl.

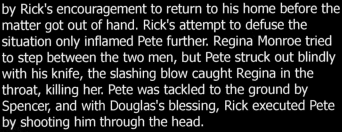

Separated from his wife and child and relocated into a new home, Pete became increasingly incensed by the conditions Rick's intervention had imposed upon him. With a knife in hand, he stalked through the streets of Alexandria and confronted Rick at Scott's burial.

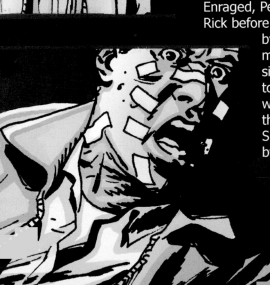

Enraged, Pete lashed out, demanding that Douglas execute Rick before he himself was forced to do so. His request was met by Rick's encouragement to return to his home before the matter got out of hand. Rick's attempt to defuse the situation only inflamed Pete further. Regina Monroe tried to step between the two men, but Pete struck out blindly with his knife, the slashing blow caught Regina in the throat, killing her. Pete was tackled to the ground by Spencer, and with Douglas's blessing, Rick executed Pete by shooting him through the head.

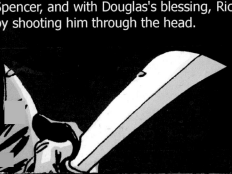

RACHEL

FIRST APPEARANCE: #10
LAST APPEARANCE: #15

STATUS: **DECEASED**
FORMER OCCUPATION: **FARM HAND**
CURRENT ROLE: **FARM HAND**
RELATIONS/ASSOCIATIONS: **DAUGHTER TO HERSHEL, SISTER TO LACEY**
ARNOLD, MAGGIE, BILLY, SUSIE
POINT OF ORIGIN: **INTRODUCED AT THE GREENE FAMILY FARM**
POINT OF DEPARTURE: **DECAPITATED BY THOMAS AT PRISON**

SAFETY BEHIND BARS:

Rachel and her twin sister Susie were Hershel Greene's youngest children. They had relocated from their farm along with the surviving members of their family (including older brother Billy and sister Maggie) to the newly discovered prison sanctuary.

The girls' disappearance one afternoon prompted Hershel to go searching the prison halls for them. Figuring that the gunfire in the gymnasium had spooked the young girls, Hershel learned from Maggie that Rachel and Susie might have sought refuge in the prison barbershop.

When he finally located the room, he discovered Rachel and Susie's decapitated bodies lying on the blood-soaked tiles. Maggie had trailed her father during his search and discovered Hershel on his knees in the doorway, the sight of his murdered daughters leaving him too distraught to speak. What they witnessed next horrified them further: Rachel and Susie's severed heads reanimated.

Billy and Glenn became concerned by Maggie and Hershel's disappearance during their efforts to cleanse the gym of the undead. The pair frantically scoured the prison. Their search led them to the barbershop where Maggie and Hershel remained, overwhelmed by their discovery. Billy consoled his sister while Glenn bravely entered the room and put a bullet into each of the girls' heads, mercifully terminating them both.

The identity of the killer immediately plunged the survivors into tension-filled chaos as accusations were leveled at Dexter, a former inmate and confessed murderer. At gunpoint, Lori and Dale forced Dexter into a cell. Their hasty actions would prove to be a costly error in judgement.

REGINA

FIRST APPEARANCE:
LAST APPEARANCE:

STATUS: DECEASED
FORMER OCCUPATION: WIFE/MOTHER
CURRENT ROLE: WIFE/MOTHER
RELATIONS/ASSOCIATIONS: WIFE TO DOUGLAS, MOTHER TO SPENCER
POINT OF ORIGIN: OBJECTED TO THE SURVIVORS ENTRY TO ALEXANDRIA
POINT OF DEPARTURE: THROAT WAS SLASHED BY PETE

LIFE AMONG THEM:

As the wife of Alexandria's leader, Regina Monroe vehemently objected to Rick and his fellow survivors' arrival. She questioned Douglas's judgment when he suggested that Rick may well be their salvation when considering his survival abilities. Regina stood her ground against her husband, and rebuffed Douglas's optimism with the notion that the new survivors so strong in numbers and experience, could simply overpower them all. Despite their disagreement, Douglas was able to reassure Regina that Rick was worthy of his confidence and her trust.

Regina's assertive nature cost her her life at the hands of Pete Anderson, an Alexandria resident whom Rick had exposed as a physically abusive husband and father. Pete was looking for revenge against Rick, and sought him out at Scott's burial. Regina tried to step between the two men after Pete threatened Rick at knifepoint. Lashing out in frustration, Pete slashed Regina's throat. Despite Spencer's best efforts to stop the attack, she was mortally wounded.

Regina's subsequent death drove Douglas into a deep fit of depression, and thus triggered his decision to place the leadership of Alexandria in Rick's hands.

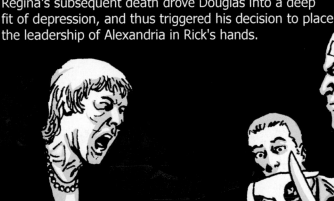

RICK

FIRST APPEARANCE: #1
LAST APPEARANCE: NA

STATUS: LIVING
FORMER OCCUPATION: POLICE OFFICER
CURRENT ROLE: CONSTABLE & LEADER OF ALEXANDRIA
RELATIONS/ASSOCIATIONS: FATHER TO CARL AND JUDITH, HUSBAND TO LORI, SHANE,
MICHONNE, ABRAHAM, TYREESE, DOUGLAS, GOVERNOR
POINT OF ORIGIN: HARRISON MEMORIAL HOSPITAL
POINT OF DEPARTURE: UNDETERMINED

DAYS GONE BYE:

Nothing could stop Rick Grimes, a small town police officer, from reuniting with his family.
Not a gunshot shot wound to the chest, nor waking from a subsequent coma into a world overrun with
the dead, nor a lonely and harrowing journey from Cynthiana, KY, to the walker-infested streets of
Atlanta. He had assistance along the way, from Morgan, who helped orient him to the realities of life
with dead, to Glenn, whose timely appearance saved Rick from a walker swarm in downtown Atlanta.

Rick reunited with his wife, Lori, and son, Carl, and to his surprise, his former police partner, Shane,
who had helped Rick's family flee to safety. Shane was loath to give up his role as Lori's partner, and his
jealousy led to his death after Carl shot him in defense of his father.

MILES BEHIND US:

A fatal attack upon the group convinced Rick of the need
to find a more defensible and permanent shelter. He led the
group onto the open road. Their ranks grew once Rick allowed
Tyreese's trio of survivors to join in the search. When Carl was
shot, Rick was taken to Hershel Greene's farm so Carl could
receive medical care. The survivors received temporary shelter
and food while Carl healed, but were forced to leave the farm
when Rick and Hershel had a falling out. As the survivors
wandered, their hopes dwindled, until Dale and Andrea
discovered a prison, which Rick immediately deemed their
new home, recognizing the potential of the security fences
and ample land for farming.

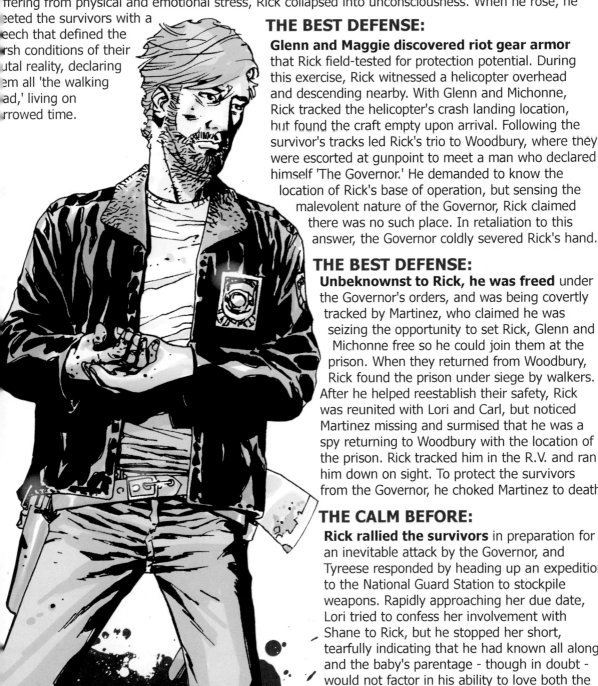

AFETY BEHIND BARS:

on after Lori announced her pregnancy, Rick and Tyreese secured the prison grounds. They
scovered four surviving inmates, and warily decided to cohabitate with them. Leadership took a toll
on Rick, and though he relocated Hershel and his family to the prison, Rick returned to Shane's
ave to terminate his undead partner (which was as much out of duty as lingering spite). Upon his
turn, Rick savagely beat Thomas near to death after discovering he killed Hershel's twin daughters.

HE HEART'S DESIRE:

hen Dexter tried to oust Rick and the survivors from the prison, Rick deftly defended their
ht to stay by shooting Dexter during a firefight with the walkers that had been loosed from Cell Block
Despite all the effort to protect his fellow survivors, the body count began to pile up around Rick. Allen
s lost to a biter attack and Carol attempted suicide, an act Rick held Tyreese accountable for following
eir breakup. The accusation led to a brutal fistfight between the two men that left both severely injured.
ffering from physical and emotional stress, Rick collapsed into unconsciousness. When he rose, he

eted the survivors with a
eech that defined the
rsh conditions of their
utal reality, declaring
em all 'the walking
ad,' living on
rrowed time.

THE BEST DEFENSE:

Glenn and Maggie discovered riot gear armor
that Rick field-tested for protection potential. During
this exercise, Rick witnessed a helicopter overhead
and descending nearby. With Glenn and Michonne,
Rick tracked the helicopter's crash landing location,
but found the craft empty upon arrival. Following the
survivor's tracks led Rick's trio to Woodbury, where they
were escorted at gunpoint to meet a man who declared
himself 'The Governor.' He demanded to know the
location of Rick's base of operation, but sensing the
malevolent nature of the Governor, Rick claimed
there was no such place. In retaliation to this
answer, the Governor coldly severed Rick's hand.

THE BEST DEFENSE:

Unbeknownst to Rick, he was freed under
the Governor's orders, and was being covertly
tracked by Martinez, who claimed he was
seizing the opportunity to set Rick, Glenn and
Michonne free so he could join them at the
prison. When they returned from Woodbury,
Rick found the prison under siege by walkers.
After he helped reestablish their safety, Rick
was reunited with Lori and Carl, but noticed
Martinez missing and surmised that he was a
spy returning to Woodbury with the location of
the prison. Rick tracked him in the R.V. and ran
him down on sight. To protect the survivors
from the Governor, he choked Martinez to death.

THE CALM BEFORE:

Rick rallied the survivors in preparation for
an inevitable attack by the Governor, and
Tyreese responded by heading up an expedition
to the National Guard Station to stockpile
weapons. Rapidly approaching her due date,
Lori tried to confess her involvement with
Shane to Rick, but he stopped her short,
tearfully indicating that he had known all along,
and the baby's parentage - though in doubt -
would not factor in his ability to love both the
child and Lori. Shortly thereafter, Lori gave birth
to Judith. Their joy was cut short when Rick
had to perform an emergency amputation on
Dale after he was bitten by a walker.

MADE TO SUFFER:

In repelling the Governor's initial attack upon the prison, Rick was shot in the abdomen.
The Governor's second attack cost Rick everything. Lori, Judith and a number of survivors were killed
the battle, while several others deserted or scattered in the aftermath, leaving Carl and a badly injure
Rick to wander the surrounding area in search of shelter.

HERE WE REMAIN:

Carl was forced to defend the house they'd settled in while his
father struggled through an infection and fever from his gunshot wound.
Once he finally regained consciousness and the ability to walk,
Rick began receiving mysterious phone calls. When the
conversations progressed over a series of reoccurring calls, Rick
learned the voice on the other end was Lori. He also learned
their calls were a figment of his disintegrating rationality. Rick
immediately rounded up supplies and left in a battered El Camino.
They stopped to scavenge gas from an abandoned truck, and Carl
was attacked by a roamer. Michonne reappeared, and saved him
from being devoured. She then joined them on their journey.
From that point, the survivors grew again in number as Rick
reunited with Glenn, Maggie, Andrea and Dale. New survivors
swelled their ranks further when a trio of new travelers headed up
by Abraham Ford persuaded Rick's group to go with them to Washington, D.C., in search of salvation

WHAT WE BECOME:

After a detour to Cynthiana, KY, to retrieve Morgan, Abraham, Rick and Carl nearly lost their live
when they were ambushed by a trio of marauders. With the threat of Carl being raped before him,
Rick killed one attacker by ripping out the man's jugular with his teeth. An emaciated and nearly-
deranged Morgan was located living in the same location as their initial meeting, though Duane
had turned undead. Rick convinced a distraught Morgan to join them. On their return journey,
they were swarmed by the largest herd of walkers any of them had witnessed. They had no choice
but to flee on foot and hastily forced the waiting members of their party on the road.

FEAR THE HUNTERS:

The journey to Washington, D.C. meant having to deal with the deaths of longtime
fellow survivors Ben, Billy and Dale. Prior to reaching Father Gabriel's church, Dale was abducted
by cannibals. When he was returned to the church, Rick used what little information he had to
track the group back to their shelter. Planting Andrea out of sight, Rick confronted the hunters.
Two precise shots from Andrea's rifle subdued their desire to retaliate. When they surrendered
their weapons, Rick executed the entire group. He wrestled
internally with his descent into savagery and confessed his
remorse to who he thought was Abraham standing over
his shoulder at Dale's funeral pyre. Rick compared
himself against Dale; how bravely, even stubbornly the
elder man had clung to his humanity and how Rick himself
had done just the opposite. When Rick turned, he realized
it had been Carl listening all the while. Seeing
tears well in his father's eyes, feeling his
shame, Carl confessed to murdering Ben.

LIFE AMONG THEM:

Rick was as shocked and saddened to learn that Eugene Porter's claim of communicating with officials in D.C. - the impetus for their journey - was nothing more than an elaborate fabrication. Rick insisted that they press on, but his discussion with Abraham over the matter was cut short when Alexandria scout Aaron revealed himself. In the aftermath of the cannibal attacks, Rick was understandably suspicious of Aaron's claims of a safe haven, but nonetheless accepted his invitation. The survivors fought their way through the walker-choked streets of D.C., and found safety at last behind Alexandria's massive security wall. Many of Rick's group were immediately assimilated into the community, and assigned duties, including Rick, who was appointed Alexandria's constable by its leader, Douglas Monroe.

TOO FAR GONE:

As Alexandria's constable, Rick was joined by Michonne, patrolling the streets, inspecting the perimeter, and keeping a watchful eye on their fellow citizens. Rick's police instincts heightened his suspicion of one member of the community in particular: Pete, whose son Rick had spotted immediately upon his arrival at Alexandria. Ron, Pete's son, had a black eye, and gave an uncertain and somewhat vague answer when Rick questioned him about the cause of the wound. Rick soon learned that Pete had been routinely abusing both Ron and his mother, Jessie. Rick and Pete came to blows, and the conflict led to the eventual death of Regina Monroe as well as Pete's execution. The gunshot that Rick fired to kill Pete had massive repercussions, and drew both a small group of violent scavengers to the gates of Alexandria, as well as a massive herd of walkers. Rick repelled the scavengers' demand of entry to the community, but he could not fend off the walkers growing in number against Alexandria's walls.

NO WAY OUT:

Pete and Regina's deaths triggered a number of consequences. Douglas abdicated leadership of Alexandria to Rick and went into seclusion. Jessie and Ron, Pete's family, took up residence with Rick and Carl, and the two adults formed an intimate bond. As the snow began to fall, so did the wall, when a seam burst and a panel gave way, allowing walkers to cascade into the streets. Rick scrambled to mount a defense, but their ranks where immediately thinned with Tobin's death and Morgan's mortal wound. The survivors retreated to their homes, and Rick formed a plan of escape. Camouflaged in walker-smeared ponchos and rain slickers, Rick led Jessie, Ron, Carl and Michonne to the gates and toward escape. Their plan failed when Ron began to cry out. They were swarmed, and Rick was forced to extremes when he severed Jessie's hand with an axe to free Carl from her grip.

Douglas appeared in the midst of the melee and began firing wild shots into the teeming walker masses. As he was devoured, a stray shot from his gun clipped Carl in the head. Rick frantically rushed to Doctor Cloyd for aid and then returned to the streets armed only with his axe and a sword-wielding Michonne at his back. Together, they made a desperate stand that inspired the other survivors (watching fearfully from the safety of their homes) to help. One by one, they emerged, weapons at the ready, each emboldened by Rick and Michonne's courage until together they eliminated the first wave of the dead. Their efforts triggered an epiphany for Rick. He gathered the remaining survivors for a meeting. With great remorse over his former actions and leadership decisions that led to countless lost survivors, Rick proclaimed they would no longer run, hide or cower. They would rebuild Alexandria's walls, expand the community and strengthen their numbers. Later that evening, as he sat at Carl's bedside, he told his son the same, and promised a secure future, one that would be filled with optimism and hope - should Carl live to see it.

RON

FIRST APPEARANCE: #70
LAST APPEARANCE: #82

STATUS: **LIVING**
FORMER OCCUPATION: **N/A**
CURRENT ROLE: **N/A**
RELATIONS/ASSOCIATIONS: **SON TO PETE & JESSIE**
POINT OF ORIGIN: **RICK NOTICED RON'S BLACK EYE UPON ENTERING ALEXANDRIA**
POINT OF DEPARTURE: **DEVOURED BY WALKERS TRYING TO ESCAPE ALEXANDRIA**

LIFE AMONG THEM:

Young Ron was spotted by Rick within moments of his arrival at Alexandria. Ron was playing football in the street with a few other children. His swollen, blackened eye immediately alerted Rick that something may be amiss.

TOO FAR GONE:

Later when Rick discovered Ron's father Pete asleep on the porch one morning during a patrol, Pete dismissed the bruise as the result of typical childhood recklessness. Unconvinced by Pete's explanation, Rick next visited Ron's mother Jessie and coaxed the truth from her: Pete had been abusing them both.

Ron and his mother Jessie eventually lived under Rick's care after a confrontation between Pete and Rick culminated in Pete's murdering Regina Monroe, and thus, his own execution.

NO WAY OUT:

Their tenure together was short-lived, when the deteriorating walls of Alexandria forced Rick to devise a plan of escape. Cloaked in the scent of the undead, Ron followed Rick, Carl and his mother Jessie, hand in hand through the walker-infested streets of Alexandria. His nerve quickly broke, and he began to panic, calling out to return home. His pleas drew the attention of the nearby walkers. Ron was instantly swarmed and devoured. Ron's fate set off a chain reaction of events that resulted in Jessie's death when she refused to release her grip upon her dying son. She too was hauled down by the undead and devoured in the streets of Alexandria.

ROSITA

FIRST APPEARANCE: #53
LAST APPEARANCE: NA

STATUS: LIVING
FORMER OCCUPATION: N/A
CURRENT ROLE: PARTNER TO ABRAHAM
RELATIONS/ASSOCIATIONS: ABRAHAM, EUGENE
POINT OF ORIGIN: INTRODUCED AS A MEMBER OF ABRAHAM'S TRIO OF WANDERERS
POINT OF DEPARTURE: UNDETERMINED

HERE WE REMAIN:

Rosita Espinosa was part of a trio of travelers making their way to Washington, D.C., when they crossed paths with the survivors at the Greene family farm. Rosita was more than a traveling companion; she was also Abraham's lover. She offered him solace and comfort following his wife's death, often soothing him when his confidence faltered. Abraham had shown a sensitivity to circumstances which had required him to kill in order to protect himself and his fellow travelers from harm, and in private moments, Rosita had been his shoulder to lean on.

NO WAY OUT:

Her trust of Abraham was shattered after their arrival at Alexandria. Once settled into the 'safe zone' Abraham struck up a relationship with Holly, a fellow construction crew member. In the aftermath of the Alexandria walker invasion, which Rosita helped repel by taking to the streets armed with a baseball bat, she revealed her knowledge of Abraham's affair with Holly, and left him. She then took up residence with Eugene Porter.

SCOTT

FIRST APPEARANCE: #69
LAST APPEARANCE: #77

STATUS: DECEASED
FORMER OCCUPATION: UNKNOWN
CURRENT ROLE: SCOUT/SUPPLY RUNNER FOR ALEXANDRIA
RELATIONS/ASSOCIATIONS: HEATH, DOCTOR CLOYD
POINT OF ORIGIN: AFTER PLUNGING FROM A BUILDING, SCOTT SEVERELY INJURED HIS LEG
POINT OF DEPARTURE: DIED OF INFECTION

LIFE AMONG THEM:

Along with his scouting partner and supply runner Heath, Scott routinely risked his life on the walker infested streets of Washington, D.C. Attempting to jump between rooftops, Scott plummeted to the ground, severely breaking his leg and struggled to maintain consciousness.

As the walkers converged upon them, Heath managed to reach street level, and used a signal flare to mark their position. Aaron and Eric, returning from their own scouting mission with Rick and his survivors in tow, caught sight of them, and arrived in time to fend off the encroaching wave of walkers. The entire envoy was almost overwhelmed until Tobin's crew arrived. Several armed gunmen cleared their path to safety.

TOO FAR GONE:

Scott was transported back to Alexandria, and taken to the care of Doctor Cloyd. However, the severe nature of his injury led to complications. The excruciating pain, an infection and a raging fever slowly debilitated Scott's strength. Although Doctor Cloyd administered painkillers and dispatched Heath and Glenn in search of stronger antibiotics, Scott suffered for some days until he succumbed to his injury and passed away.

Before Scott's service and burial, Michonne spiked his brain to ensure he would not return from the grave.

SHANE

FIRST APPEARANCE: #2
LAST APPEARANCE: #6

STATUS: DECEASED
FORMER OCCUPATION: POLICE OFFICER, RICK'S PARTNER
CURRENT ROLE: ORIGINAL CAMP MEMBER
RELATIONS/ASSOCIATIONS: RICK, LORI, CARL, DALE, ALLEN, JIM, ANDREA, AMY
POINT OF ORIGIN: SHANE HELPED ESCORT LORI AND CARL TO ATLANTA
POINT OF DEPARTURE: SHANE WAS SHOT BY CARL IN DEFENSE OF HIS FATHER

DAYS GONE BYE:

Shane was Rick's former partner, serving on the Cynthiana Police Force. He escorted Rick's wife, Lori, and son, Carl, to the promised safety of Atlanta after the dead began to rise. They never reached the city, but found comfort in each other's arms while on the road. Though remorseful for advancing himself sexually upon Lori, Shane admitted to wanting her for a long time prior to their night together on the outskirts of the fallen city.

The trio joined a number of other survivors in a makeshift camp and formed the original survivor group. Shane assumed a leadership role, and advised the group to remain in place, believing firmly that they would be well positioned when the military arrived in Atlanta. Rick's miraculous reappearance brought Shane and Lori's relationship to an abrupt end, an adjustment Shane struggled to handle calmly. Slowly, Rick's presence and natural leadership skills inflamed Shane's jealousy, and filled him with a gnawing anger.

His emotions clouded his judgment, and this endangered the group. When Rick suggested a camp relocation, Shane vigorously objected. He soon became irrational in his persistence to remain in place, and directly thereafter the camp was attacked. Amy was killed, and Jim was mortally injured. Still, Shane would not relent, and he punched Rick for insinuating the attack was his fault.

During a hunting trip into the surrounding woods, Shane grew increasingly agitated. He made continuous references to Lori and the life he would never have now that Rick had reappeared. In a fit of rage and emotion, Shane trained his rifle upon Rick. A shot rang out. Shane's neck burst in a spray of blood. Carl had trailed the men into the woods. Seeing his father a flinch away from being murdered, he fired with the gun Rick had given him, and killed Shane.

Rick later returned to Shane's grave, exhumed his undead body, and put a bullet through his head. Though it was never medically determined, Shane's legacy proved to be the birth of Judith Grimes.

SOPHIA

FIRST APPEARANCE: #2
LAST APPEARANCE: NA

STATUS: LIVING
FORMER OCCUPATION: N/A
CURRENT ROLE: IN CARE OF GLENN & MAGGIE
RELATIONS/ASSOCIATIONS: DAUGHTER OF JIM & CAROL, MAGGIE, GLENN, CARL
POINT OF ORIGIN: ORIGINAL CAMP MEMBER
POINT OF DEPARTURE: UNDETERMINED

DAYS GONE BYE:

Like many of the fellow survivors, young Sophia had experienced her fair share of loss. Her father killed himself shortly after the dead rose. Sophia and her mother Carol attempted to reach Atlanta to stay with Sophia's aunt, but stopped short as the city fell to the undead. The pair discovered Dale's camp and joined the other survivors.

MILES BEHIND US:

While Carol appeared to find love with Tyreese, Sophia warmed to Carl Grimes. Recuperating from a gunshot wound, Sophia planted an affectionate kiss upon Carl's cheek, telling him his new scar was 'sexy.'

THE HEART'S DESIRE:

Entrenched at the prison, Sophia further acclimated to the undead now surrounding her from every side. Staring out through the chain-link fences holding the walkers at bay, Sophia confessed to Carl that she no longer feared the walkers, but rather felt sorry for them, because they appeared 'sad.' While Sophia and Carl's friendship blossomed, her mother struggled to find new companionship after her relationship with Tyreese dissolved due to Michonne's arrival.

THE CALM BEFORE:

Carl got his chance to return Sophia's affection soon after a despondent Carol sacrificed herself to a chained-up biter in the prison yard. Carol's death left Sophia emotionally shattered and mute. Even Carl's gentle prodding could not pierce her wide-eyed silence. Lori assumed temporary care of Sophia, and with Carl's persistence, Sophia slowly emerged from her shock.

MADE TO SUFFER - NO WAY OUT:

Dale made the first of two vital decisions that saved Sophia's life. Prior to the deadly raid upon the prison, he forcibly removed Sophia from Lori's care and left before the Governor's forces slaughtered many of the survivors.

Sophia fell into Maggie and Glenn's care, making the journey with them to Alexandria. Maggie very astutely understood that fleeing the safety of their home would lead to their deaths when the walkers overran the safety barrier. She kept Sophia with her as others perished in the street outside their home.

SPENCER

FIRST APPEARANCE: #72
LAST APPEARANCE: NA

STATUS: LIVING
FORMER OCCUPATION: UNKNOWN
CURRENT ROLE: UNKNOWN
RELATIONS/ASSOCIATIONS: SON TO DOUGLAS & REGINA
POINT OF ORIGIN: INTRODUCED HIMSELF TO ANDREA AT AN EVENING PARTY
POINT OF DEPARTURE: UNDETERMINED

LIFE AMONG THEM:

Spencer Monroe began his courtship with Andrea at an evening meet and greet party that the Alexandria residents hosted for the new arrivals. He flattered her with comments about her sharp-shooting skills, and encouraged her to offer a demonstration to the other residents.

TOO FAR GONE:

Andrea later joined Spencer at his new home. An offer for dinner enticed her, but it was apparent Andrea had taken an immediate liking to Spencer. They nearly kissed, but Andrea broke off their embrace, and she tearfully explained that there had recently been 'another man' who had died, and maybe it was too soon for another relationship. Spencer acknowledged his understanding of Andrea's feelings, and insisted they enjoy dinner together and nothing more. Their dinner date was cut short when Andrea witnessed Pete walking down the street with a knife drawn. Spencer followed, and witnessed Pete slashing his mother's throat. Spencer tackled Pete to the ground in a vain attempt to save her life, but it was too late.

NO WAY OUT:

When Andrea got trapped in the bell tower outside of Alexandria, Spencer devised a slack-line for him, Glenn and Heath to shimmy across in order to ferry supplies to her. The line snapped as Spencer crossed the gap between the

wall and the tower, sending him plummeting towards the walkers below. Glenn, Heath, and Andrea hauled him to safety but with no way back.

Spencer fell out of favor with Andrea when he suggested that the two of them abandon Alexandria and the survivors trapped inside in favor of escape together. Spencer's selfish motives prompted Andrea to punch him in the face, and redouble her efforts to assist all those trapped by the walker swarm inside Alexandria's walls.

Despite Spencer's poorly timed proposition, he has remained by Andrea's side as the foursome returned to Alexandria to assist in the survival of their fellow residents.

SUSIE

FIRST APPEARANCE:
LAST APPEARANCE:

STATUS: DECEASED
FORMER OCCUPATION: **FARM HAND**
CURRENT ROLE: **FARM HAND**
RELATIONS/ASSOCIATIONS: **DAUGHTER TO HERSHEL, SISTER TO ARNOLD, LACEY, MAGGIE, BILLY, RACHEL, THOMAS**
POINT OF ORIGIN: **INTRODUCED AT THE GREENE FAMILY FARM**
POINT OF DEPARTURE: **DECAPITATED BY THOMAS IN PRISON**

THIS SORROWFUL LIFE:

Susie, along with her twin sister, Rachel were the youngest members of the Greene family. Their lives were cut short at the hands of Thomas, a former inmate and resident of the prison the survivors had chosen to inhabit when it was deemed a suitable stronghold.

When Susie and Rachel were discovered decapitated in the prison barbershop by their father Hershel, chaos reigned. Confessed murderer Dexter was falsely accused of their double murder, and confined to a cell against his will. When Susie and Rachel's severed heads reanimated, Glenn shot them both in the head, permanently terminating the sisters. Meanwhile, the surviving Greene family members grieved the loss of the sisters.

With Dexter imprisoned, the attacks continued. Thomas revealed himself as the killer when he made another attempt, this time on Andrea in the laundry station. She fought Thomas off and fled into the prison yard, her killer in pursuit. Rick spotted them and subdued Thomas, beating him within inches of his life.

Thomas was to be hanged upon Rick's orders, but a sympathetic Patricia attempted to free him before his execution. Thomas turned on her and their scuffle brought Tyreese and Maggie to the scene.

Maggie exacted a measure of revenge and justice for Susie and Rachel's murder when she shot Thomas multiple times at close range, killing him.

THERESA

FIRST APPEARANCE: #53
LAST APPEARANCE: #66

STATUS: **DECEASED**
FORMER OCCUPATION: **UNKNOWN**
CURRENT ROLE: **HUNTER/CANNIBAL**
RELATIONS/ASSOCIATIONS: **ALBERT, GREG, CHRIS, DAVID**
POINT OF ORIGIN: **REVEALED AS A CANNIBAL AFTER DALE'S ABDUCTION**
POINT OF DEPARTURE: **KILLED BY ABRAHAM, ANDREA, MICHONNE & RICK**

FEAR THE HUNTERS:

As a member of the cannibalistic hunting party, Theresa helped stalk Rick's group as they took temporary shelter nearby.

The hunters decided to strike Dale when he abandoned his fellow survivors to die from a roamer bite in private. They abducted Dale, then amputated and cooked his lower leg over an open fire. When he later regained consciousness, Dale revealed that he'd been bitten and was 'tainted meat.' In their revulsion, the cannibals panicked. David proved the voice of reason, suggesting they all remain calm - a point Theresa was quick to support.

The hunters returned Dale to the other survivors, dumping his unconscious body outside Father Gabriel's church. Theresa and her follow hunters paid the price for their assault upon Dale when Rick tracked them back to their base camp.

After demonstrating their superior strength, Rick and several accompanying survivors forced the hunters to surrender. Their guns were confiscated, and Theresa, along with the other five members of her party, was executed. To ensure they would not return as the undead, their bodies were burned.

THOMAS

FIRST APPEARANCE:
LAST APPEARANCE:

STATUS: **DECEASED**
FORMER OCCUPATION: **UNKNOWN**
CURRENT ROLE: **INMATE**
RELATIONS/ASSOCIATIONS: **ANDREW, AXEL, DEXTER, RACHEL & SUSIE, ANDREA, RICK**
POINT OF ORIGIN: **DISCOVERED IN THE PRISON CAFETERIA BY RICK & TYREESE**
POINT OF DEPARTURE: **SHOT BY MAGGIE SEVERAL TIMES**

SAFETY BEHIND BARS:

One of four convicts discovered in the prison cafeteria by Rick and Tyreese as they scouted the grounds for biters, Thomas claimed he was imprisoned for tax fraud, an indictment he also claimed was not the result of his wrongdoing. He offered little more; he was a man of few words and even less desire to integrate with the new prison residents.

Although not evident at first, Thomas's claim was a sham - he was a psychopathic murderer, and decapitated Hershel Greene's twin daughters, Rachel and Susie. When his fellow former inmate Dexter was wrongly accused of the crime, Thomas was allowed to continue his attacks, next cornering Andrea in an empty laundry station. Thomas gashed her cheek from mouth to ear, but Andrea was able to escape. With his knife drawn, Thomas gave chase, pursuing Andrea out into the prison yard, where he was spotted and apprehended by Rick.

Thomas was severely beaten to near death before Tyreese pulled Rick from his battered body. Upon Rick's order, Thomas was taken back to a cell in preparation for his hanging the following morning.

Unable to see another human being killed, Patricia tried to sneak Thomas out of his cell in an ill-fated attempt to set him free. He turned on Patricia, and tried to choke her to death.

She clawed his face, and in doing so, she freed herself. The resulting noise from their scuffle brought Tyreese and Maggie rushing to the cell. When Thomas did not surrender himself at Tyreese's request, Maggie fired on Thomas. Several shots to his midsection dropped him to his knees. Several more shots to the back of his head finished Thomas. His body was placed outside the prison fences where it was consumed by scores of lurking walkers.

TOBIN

LAST APPEARANCE:

STATUS **DECEASED**
FORMER OCCUPATION: **UNKNOWN**
CURRENT ROLE: **CONSTRUCTION CREW CHIEF, ALEXANDRIA**
RELATIONS/ASSOCIATIONS: **ABRAHAM, BRUCE, DOUGLAS, HOLLY**
POINT OF ORIGIN: **INTRODUCED TO ABRAHAM AS HIS CREW SUPERVISOR**
POINT OF DEPARTURE: **DEVOURED BY WALKERS WHEN THE WALL COLLAPSED**

TOO FAR GONE:

As the chief of Alexandria's construction crew, Tobin was in charge of the maintenance and expansion of the safety barrier that protected the citizens within from the undead lurking outside. The strain of both guarding the crew and constructing the wall took its toll upon him. Tobin failed to react swiftly to a walker attack upon Holly that left her cut off from assistance and facing certain death Abraham - well versed in self-defense, and having spent several months on the road - stepped in and helped clear the way to safety.

Both Abraham and Holly held Tobin accountable for his conservative system of defense that jeopardized their lives. This incident rattled Tobin, and eroded his confidence to the point that he relinquished his title as chief, allowing Abraham to lead the crew. In a private meeting with Douglas, Tobin revealed that he was no longer the crew chief, and admitted that his leadership may have led to the loss of several lives during the creation of the wall. Furthermore, he indicated that Abraham was far more suited to the rigors of the position, given his survival experience.

NO WAY OUT:

Tobin died defending Alexandria when a seam in the security wall buckled and a panel collapsed, allowing a stream of walkers into the community. As the invasion began, he stood guard along the wall, fighting off as many biters as possible, allowing Holly to summon help. She returned with reinforcements, but Tobin had been over-whelmed, and his eviscerated body lay feet from the compromised wall he helped to build.

TYREESE

FIRST APPEARANCE: #7
LAST APPEARANCE: #48

STATUS: DECEASED
FORMER OCCUPATION: NFL LINEBACKER, BOUNCER, CAR SALESMAN
CURRENT ROLE: RICK'S LEADERSHIP PARTNER
RELATIONS/ASSOCIATIONS: FATHER OF JULIE, CHRIS, RICK, MICHONNE, GOVERNOR
POINT OF ORIGIN: STUMBLED UPON THE SURVIVORS PRIOR TO THE PRISON
POINT OF DEPARTURE: DECAPITATED BY THE GOVERNOR WITH MICHONNE'S SWORD

MILES BEHIND US:

Tyreese, with his daughter, Julie and her boyfriend, Chris, had been living together before and after the dead began to rise. The trio soon ran out of food. Starving and freezing, Tyreese, armed only with a hammer, led them in search of sustenance. They stumbled upon Rick and his fellow survivors as they were clearing the roadway of an abandoned vehicle. In the darkness, Rick almost mistook them for walkers. Mercifully, Rick provided food for Tyreese's trio and took an instant liking to their leader, a former Atlanta Falcons linebacker.

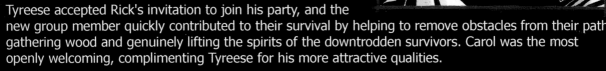

Tyreese accepted Rick's invitation to join his party, and the new group member quickly contributed to their survival by helping to remove obstacles from their path, gathering wood and genuinely lifting the spirits of the downtrodden survivors. Carol was the most openly welcoming, complimenting Tyreese for his more attractive qualities.

Upon arriving at the Wiltshire Estates, Tyreese helped clear out a home of lurking biters and saved Rick from an attack. Settling in for the evening, Carol volunteered to share a room with Tyreese. The following morning, the pair awoke in each other's arms. Despite being a gated community, the Wiltshire Estates was infested with roamers. Tyreese scrambled to help the survivors escape, and in the panic found Julie and Chris sexually engaged. They made a hasty rooftop exit onto the roof of the R.V. and bolted from the housing complex for the open road.

After locating the prison, Tyreese and Rick secured the area, clearing the grounds of the remaining walkers. The group had hopes of making the prison their permanent shelter. Tyreese disagreed with Rick's decision to ask Hershel to join them, but acted as the leader in his absence. He soon had other more grave concerns as Julie and Chris executed their suicide pact. When Chris murdered Julie, Tyreese rushed to his daughter's aid, but could do nothing more than cradle her dead body in his arms. When she turned undead, Tyreese struggled with his emotions, pleading for a chance to somehow resurrect Julie's humanity by reasoning with her. Chris shot Julie again, permanently terminating her, and Tyreese then turned his full fury upon Chris, strangling him to death. He warned Rick to leave him, because when Chris returned

from the dead Tyreese planned to kill him again, only more slowly. The following morning, Tyreese burned their bodies in the yard as promised. Rick was unnerved by his eerily calm demeanor.

Shortly thereafter, Tyreese gathered Andrea, Billy and Glenn, with the desired goal of clearing out a walker-filled gymnasium. The foursome entered fully armed, firing upon scores of undead shuffling about. Tyreese waded into the thick of the horde and was overwhelmed. Forced into a retreat, his companions bolted through the doors and locked them, leaving him for dead. When Rick returned from a trip to Shane's grave, he investigated the gym only to find Tyreese reclining quietly in a corner. Exhausted, he had killed every last walker with a handgun and hammer.

The event seemed to give Tyreese some clarity. He grew more intimate with Carol, confided his feelings to Rick, and intervened as the voice of reason after Thomas's murder of Rachel and Susie, by demanding the establishment of rules in order to stabilize the group's behavioral expectations. Tyreese's life radically changed once more with Michonne's arrival. She recalled him from his playing days with the Falcons, and the pair struck up an immediate kinship over football and weightlifting. After a fight with Rick about amputating Allen's walker-bitten leg, Tyreese went to the gym to relieve the tension. Michonne found him there and offered oral sex. Unbeknownst to them both, Carol was watching tearfully through the gymnasium window.

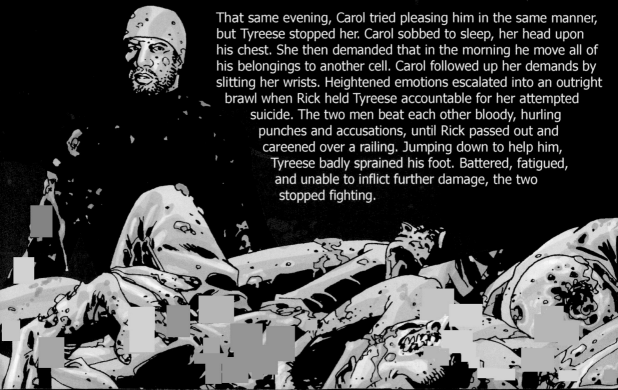

That same evening, Carol tried pleasing him in the same manner, but Tyreese stopped her. Carol sobbed to sleep, her head upon his chest. She then demanded that in the morning he move all of his belongings to another cell. Carol followed up her demands by slitting her wrists. Heightened emotions escalated into an outright brawl when Rick held Tyreese accountable for her attempted suicide. The two men beat each other bloody, hurling punches and accusations, until Rick passed out and careened over a railing. Jumping down to help him, Tyreese badly sprained his foot. Battered, fatigued, and unable to inflict further damage, the two stopped fighting.

Not long after the two combatants recovered, Rick, Glenn and Michonne went missing after searching for a downed helicopter. Clad in riot gear, Tyreese searched the surrounding country side on foot. He returned to the prison empty-handed.

When Rick, Michonne and Glenn finally returned in far wors condition, Tyreese took charge of the deteriorating situation He and Alex led a party of able-bodied survivors into the ya to clear out the walkers that had invaded the grounds. He made amends with Rick regarding their falling out, and afte Carl confessed to doubting his father's love for him, Tyreese firmly consoled and reassured the emotionally fragile young boy.

THE CALM BEFORE:

The threat of attack by the Governor loomed over the survivors. Tyreese headed up an expedition to the National Guard Station to gather weapons in preparation against invasion by the Woodbury forces. The survivors obtained gas, weapons and munitions (including a milita supply truc and then detonated the base, preventing the Governor from utilizing it as a supply depo Returning to the prison, the group was ambushed by a Woodbury scouting party, but survived the confrontation. Upon returning to the prison, Tyreese and Carol's relationship came to a final and bloody end when sh sacrificed herself to a walker, and died in his arms. Carol's suicide left Tyreese guilt-ridden, but withholding of his sorrow for her. He turned his attention to preparing for the looming war with Woodbury and formed a solid bond of friendship with Andrea. He even helped her fashion a prosthetic for Dale's amputated leg. Just as Michonne began to warm to him again after her trauma in Woodbury the Governor's forces arrived at the prison fences.

MADE TO SUFFER:

The Woodbury army immediately fired upon the survivors. They rushed for cover, and Tyreese was nearly shot, but Michonne tackled him to the ground. She used his gun to return fire and create cover. When the Governor's forces retreated, Tyreese and Michonne helped aid the wounded, including Rick and Andrea. Seeking a chance to gain the advantage in the conflict, Michonne convinced Tyreese that the two of them should attack Woodbury in hopes of thinning their forces. Clad in riot gear, the pair made their way to Woodbury a a dead sprint. In the woods surrounding the prison, Michonne located Gabe and his cadre of scouts.

Tyreese and Michonne attacked. Although they managed to kill three Woodbury soldiers, the pair was overwhelmed. Tyreese was captured and Michonne's sword was confiscated. Both were presented to the Governor, and he seized upon them with a malicious purpose. Tyreese was severely beaten, then paraded in front of his fellow survivors from the back of a pickup truck. The Governor demanded that he be allowed entry to the prison, and that all within surrender. A bloodied, partially toothless Tyreese bravely called out to the prison residents to stand their ground. The Governor demonstrated the severity of his threat, and sliced the base of Tyreese's neck with Michonne's sword. He did so repeatedly, until Tyreese's head dropped free from his lifeless body.

Long after the battle for the prison concluded, Michonne returned and used her recovered sword to spike Tyreese's reanimated head, permanently terminating her lover's life.

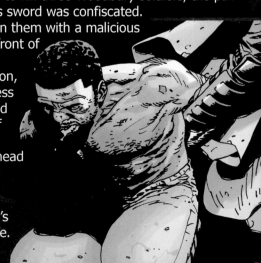

MORE GREAT BOOKS FROM ROBERT KIRKMAN & IMAGE COMICS!

THE ASTOUNDING WOLF-MAN

VOL. 1 TP
ISBN: 978-1-58240-862-0
$14.99
VOL. 2 TP
ISBN: 978-1-60706-007-9
$14.99
VOL. 3 TP
ISBN: 978-1-60706-111-3
$16.99
VOL. 4 TP
ISBN: 978-1-60706-249-3
$16.99

BATTLE POPE

VOL. 1: GENESIS TP
ISBN: 978-1-58240-572-8
$14.99
VOL. 2: MAYHEM TP
ISBN: 978-1-58240-529-2
$12.99
VOL. 3: PILLOW TALK TP
ISBN: 978-1-58240-677-0
$12.99
VOL. 4: WRATH OF GOD TP
ISBN: 978-1-58240-751-7
$9.99

BRIT

VOL. 1: OLD SOLDIER TP
ISBN: 978-1-58240-678-7
$14.99
VOL. 2: AWOL
ISBN: 978-1-58240-864-4
$14.99
VOL. 3: FUBAR
ISBN: 978-1-60706-061-1
$16.99

CAPES

VOL. 1: PUNCHING THE CLOCK TP
ISBN: 978-1-58240-756-2
$17.99

HAUNT

VOL. 1 TP
ISBN: 978-1-60706-154-0
$9.99
VOL. 2 TP
ISBN: 978-1-60706-229-5
$16.99

THE INFINITE

VOL. 1 TP
ISBN: 978-1-60706-475-6
$9.99

INVINCIBLE

VOL. 1: FAMILY MATTERS TP
ISBN: 978-1-58240-711-1
$12.99
VOL. 2: EIGHT IS ENOUGH TP
ISBN: 978-1-58240-347-2
$12.99

VOL. 3: PERFECT STRANGERS TP
ISBN: 978-1-58240-793-7
$12.99
VOL. 4: HEAD OF THE CLASS TP
ISBN: 978-1-58240-440-2
$14.95
VOL. 5: THE FACTS OF LIFE TP
ISBN: 978-1-58240-554-4
$14.99
VOL. 6: A DIFFERENT WORLD TP
ISBN: 978-1-58240-579-7
$14.99
VOL. 7: THREE'S COMPANY TP
ISBN: 978-1-58240-656-5
$14.99
VOL. 8: MY FAVORITE MARTIAN TP
ISBN: 978-1-58240-683-1
$14.99
VOL. 9: OUT OF THIS WORLD TP
ISBN: 978-1-58240-827-9
$14.99
VOL. 10: WHO'S THE BOSS TP
ISBN: 978-1-60706-013-0
$16.99
VOL. 11: HAPPY DAYS TP
ISBN: 978-1-60706-062-8
$16.99
VOL. 12: STILL STANDING TP
ISBN: 978-1-60706-166-3
$16.99
VOL. 13: GROWING PAINS TP
ISBN: 978-1-60706-251-6
$16.99
VOL. 14: THE VILTRUMITE WAR TP
ISBN: 978-1-60706-367-4
$19.99
VOL. 15: GET SMART TP
ISBN: 978-1-60706-498-5
$16.99
ULTIMATE COLLECTION, VOL. 1 HC
ISBN 978-1-58240-500-1
$34.95
ULTIMATE COLLECTION, VOL. 2 HC
ISBN: 978-1-58240-594-0
$34.99
ULTIMATE COLLECTION, VOL. 3 HC
ISBN: 978-1-58240-763-0
$34.99
ULTIMATE COLLECTION, VOL. 4 HC
ISBN: 978-1-58240-989-4
$34.99
ULTIMATE COLLECTION, VOL. 5 HC
ISBN: 978-1-60706-116-8
$34.99
ULTIMATE COLLECTION, VOL. 6 HC
ISBN: 978-1-60706-360-5
$34.99
ULTIMATE COLLECTION, VOL. 7 HC
ISBN: 978-1-60706-509-8
$39.99
THE OFFICIAL HANDBOOK OF THE INVINCIBLE UNIVERSE TP
ISBN: 978-1-58240-831-6
$12.99

INVINCIBLE PRESENTS,
VOL. 1: ATOM EVE & REX SPLODE TP
ISBN: 978-1-60706-255-4
$14.99
THE COMPLETE INVINCIBLE LIBRARY, VOL. 2 HC
ISBN: 978-1-60706-112-0
$125.00
THE COMPLETE INVINCIBLE LIBRARY, VOL. 3 HC
ISBN: 978-1-60706-421-3
$125.00
INVINCIBLE COMPENDIUM VOL. 1
ISBN: 978-1-60706-411-4
$64.99

THE WALKING DEAD

VOL. 1: DAYS GONE BYE TP
ISBN: 978-1-58240-672-5
$9.99
VOL. 2: MILES BEHIND US TP
ISBN: 978-1-58240-775-3
$14.99
VOL. 3: SAFETY BEHIND BARS TP
ISBN: 978-1-58240-805-7
$14.99
VOL. 4: THE HEART'S DESIRE TP
ISBN: 978-1-58240-530-8
$14.99
VOL. 5: THE BEST DEFENSE TP
ISBN: 978-1-58240-612-1
$14.99
VOL. 6: THIS SORROWFUL LIFE TP
ISBN: 978-1-58240-684-8
$14.99
VOL. 7: THE CALM BEFORE TP
ISBN: 978-1-58240-828-6
$14.99
VOL. 8: MADE TO SUFFER TP
ISBN: 978-1-58240-883-5
$14.99
VOL. 9: HERE WE REMAIN TP
ISBN: 978-1-60706-022-2
$14.99
VOL. 10: WHAT WE BECOME TP
ISBN: 978-1-60706-075-8
$14.99
VOL. 11: FEAR THE HUNTERS TP
ISBN: 978-1-60706-181-6
$14.99
VOL. 12: LIFE AMONG THEM TP
ISBN: 978-1-60706-254-7
$14.99
VOL. 13: TOO FAR GONE TP
ISBN: 978-1-60706-329-2
$14.99
VOL. 14: NO WAY OUT TP
ISBN: 978-1-60706-392-6
$14.99
VOL. 15: WE FIND OURSELVES TP
ISBN: 978-1-60706-392-6
$14.99
BOOK ONE HC
ISBN: 978-1-58240-619-0
$34.99

BOOK TWO HC
ISBN: 978-1-58240-698-5
$34.99
BOOK THREE HC
ISBN: 978-1-58240-825-5
$34.99
BOOK FOUR HC
ISBN: 978-1-60706-000-0
$34.99
BOOK FIVE HC
ISBN: 978-1-60706-171-7
$34.99
BOOK SIX HC
ISBN: 978-1-60706-327-8
$34.99
BOOK SEVEN HC
ISBN: 978-1-60706-439-8
$34.99
DELUXE HARDCOVER, VOL. 1
ISBN: 978-1-58240-619-0
$100.00
DELUXE HARDCOVER, VOL. 2
ISBN: 978-1-60706-029-7
$100.00
DELUXE HARDCOVER, VOL. 3
ISBN: 978-1-60706-330-8
$100.00
THE WALKING DEAD: THE COVERS, VOL. 1 HC
ISBN: 978-1-60706-002-4
$24.99
THE WALKING DEAD SURVIVORS' GUIDE
ISBN: 978-1-60706-458-9
$12.99

REAPER

GRAPHIC NOVEL
ISBN: 978-1-58240-354-2
$6.95

SUPER DINOSAUR

VOL. 1
ISBN: 978-1-60706-420-6
$9.99
DELUXE COLORING BOOK
ISBN: 978-1-60706-481-7
$4.99

SUPERPATRIOT

AMERICA'S FIGHTING FORCE
ISBN: 978-1-58240-355-1
$14.99

TALES OF THE REALM

HARDCOVER
ISBN: 978-1-58240-426-0
$34.95
TRADE PAPERBACK
ISBN: 978-1-58240-394-6
$14.95

TECH JACKET

VOL. 1: THE BOY FROM EARTH TP
ISBN: 978-1-58240-771-5
$14.99

TO FIND YOUR NEAREST COMIC BOOK STORE, CALL: 1-888-COMIC-BOOK